LETTER FROM THE DEAD:

"I know what you are, Sabella. I didn't know until I came to God, but when I found God, He told me. His angels told me. I know what you've done. I know you killed my sister. I hope the cross cripples you, as it should. If it doesn't, I've made another arrangement. Don't try to guess what it is. You're just one of the wolves, Sabella, an animal, and animals can't guess things. Not till it's too late. But you don't have so long, Sabella. I hope it's soon, and then you'll rot, and your soul, if you have one, will writhe and shriek in Eternal Fires, Sabella, and God will let me hear you as I rest on His bosom."

TANITH LEE
has also written

THE BIRTHGRAVE
VAZKOR, SON OF VAZKOR
QUEST FOR THE WHITE WITCH
DON'T BITE THE SUN
DRINKING SAPPHIRE WINE
VOLKHAVAAR
NIGHT'S MASTER
DEATH'S MASTER
ELECTRIC FOREST
THE STORM LORD
DAY BY NIGHT *

* Forthcoming

SABELLA

or

The Blood Stone

Tanith Lee

DAW BOOKS, INC.
DONALD A. WOLLHEIM, PUBLISHER

1633 Broadway
New York, N.Y. 10019

Copyright ©, 1980, by Tanith Lee.

All Rights Reserved.

Cover art by George Smith.

FIRST PRINTING, APRIL 1980

1 2 3 4 5 6 7 8 9

DAW TRADEMARK REGISTERED
U.S. PAT. OFF. MARCA
REGISTRADA. HECHO EN U.S.A.

Part

ONE

The Wolves

1

I was out hunting the night my aunt Cassi died. As she was taking her last breath of revitalized Arean air, I was high on the Hammerhead Plateau, under forty thousand stars burning like diamond bonfires. Maybe I even killed in the same minute she let that last breath go. I hadn't meant to kill, perhaps it was an omen. And did I feel her reach out to me in the black eye-star-burning darkness, reach out with her dead finger, pointing, beckoning, condemning me, me thinking it was only the chill night wind of Novo Mars?

Just after sunup (Novo Mars sunup like a bomb of light going off in the sky: sixty-second dawn) the mailman buzzed the porch. He was a real man, the mailman, I mean human, because mechanization doesn't stretch out too far into the Styx of Hammerhead. He stood against the fresh pink sky, his electric mail dolly sitting beside him. When I went to open up, he saw me just as he always did, in my black wrapper and my dark glasses, my hair like black coffee poured over me from the crown of my head to my shoulders. He thinks I'm a slut, a boozy drug addict. Thinks? Thought. Maybe still thinks, who knows.

"Miss Quey? Registered stellagram. Thumbprint right here."

He looked resentful, as he always did. He was wondering if I'd seduce him someday in my silky wrapper. But I wouldn't. He thought my name Quey, (pronounced Kay) was phony too. The name on the sender's docket was Koberman, Cassi's name.

"Thanks," I said, as I thumbprinted.

"Sorry to wake you," said the mailman. His stupid sad malevolent human eyes said to me: I guess all you whores have to sleep it off in the morning.

But I didn't argue, not then, with the tepid rosewater sun streaming in my door and my hands shaking a little and the lightweight stella like a pack of lead.

"That's O.K.," I said, and buttoned shut the smoked-glass door, and slunk back into the lovely shadows.

All the blue paper day-blinds were down, and the blinds of violet cotton. How beautiful it all looked, true virtue of necessity. But that one slap of light in the face had told. I remembered the striped deer and some weak tears oozed from my eyes.

Out in the hallway, over the stair, the stained-glass window cries too, staining the wooden floor with a big crimson patch.

When I finally opened the stella, I wasn't really interested in it, it was something else that had to be seen to. At first I thought it was from Cassi herself, and wondered why she'd suddenly recollected me and what she wanted that she had to send star-bounced telegrams for, and what it was going to mean. (Does anyone else ever read their mail like this? Trepidation always, occasionally fear. How I loved ads and circulars, things you could send for or forget.) But then I found it wasn't Cassi, but Cassi's brother-in-law, a lawyer's formal bit of paper with formal phrases on it. Cassi was dead, but she'd sent me an invite to the funeral. She'd fixed her heart on it. And to ensure I came, she'd left me several thousand tax-clear New Mars credits. I hadn't recalled she was wealthy. I hadn't known she recalled where I was or even if I was still on-planet. I didn't know either what her post mortem game was, but it seemed to me she had set out to nail me on a very special Revivalist Christian Cross. But then, would she, all these years, have known that *too?*

Why does everybody have to love money so much? I wasn't rich. They'd expect me to want to be, and if I didn't, they'd want to find out why not. And Cassi had remembered where I was and they'd traced me here. Even if I ran (I contemplated that) they'd follow me.

Sabella Quey, this cash belongs to you, they'd say, as we stood there in the bright delicate sunlight of rose-hued Novo Mars.

An hour later, I went to the music deck and keyed in the phones. I let the sinister marvel of a Prokofiev symphony wash up through the house and over me as the jets of the shower washed down.

But oh, Sabella Quey, the cross stands ready.

The funeral, the day after tomorrow, drawing me, as if by suction, back into the world.

Novo Mars is enough like old Mars to have been dubbed with the name, but a pink planet rather than red, pearl rather than ruby. I was born east of Ares. This little world is all I've ever known. It's sugar-mouse color skies with their pale blue clouds of oxygen revitalization that turn the air over the cities to a lavender soup, the tawny-rose sands, the knife-ridge plateaus like pasteboard cutouts, the rust-red crags dissolving in the five-second dusks.

The vegetation is all earth-import, the books tell you, and mostly so is the fauna that breeds and hunts and basks and leaves its bones on plains and heights and in the dry canals. But both flora and fauna have mutated here to fit new climates, zones and geography. The waters were also initially false, atmospheric stabilizers replenished by viaduct and sub-surface reservoir, yet they, too, like crystal tinted by indigenous skies and pointed mountains, have become one with Novo Mars. There are genuine ruins (beware tourist traps) here and there. Thin pillars soaring, leveled foundations crumbling, cracked urns whispering of spilled dusts—all the Martian dreams that old Mars denied to mankind. Though this prior race, whose wreck men inherited, left small self-evidence beyond their architecture. Maybe men find it, anyway, more romantic to guess.

But there are still real Martian wolves in the hills above Hammerhead Plateau. Fine nights, you can hear them howl in tin-whistle voices, like antique lost locomotives searching for a station. Periodically, men come out from the cities and shoot at them, and those nights, from Brade to Hammerlake, the uplands ring to lead-blast and electric flash-gun charge. But wolves that have survived so many things, a passing of peoples, drought of four-fifths of the water, death of half the air—they can survive guns. Their rough coats are like pink champagne, their genes programmed long ago to copy the dusts, but catch the glare of their eyes at night, disembodied blood drops seemingly framed in stars, and know them for what they are.

When they cry, when they cry, Sabella, the hair lifts on the scalp, and the eyes fill up with tears and the mouth with water.

I took the night flight to Aresport. It's a two-hour run by air-bug from the Brade lift-off point. To reach Brade, there'd been the nineteen o'clock flyer from Hammerlake Halt. I'd footed the five miles to the Halt, through the fading afternoon, the scarlet minute of pre-sunset, through the seconds of sunset, through the tidal wave of night. Five miles was nothing to me, and the road was good. Once the sun went out, I took off my black straw hat and the big black glasses and carried them with my sandals and my single piece of luggage.

The half-hour flyer ride was uneventful, the bus almost empty, though we picked up a pair of couples on route through Spur and Canyon.

When I'd checked into the cabin of the air-bug at Brade and fastened myself down in the plasti-plush seat, the first intimation of fate came over me. I'd been expecting it; not such force. After all, I'd undertaken a few unavoidable journeys before, and I'd survived, sometimes with fewer scars than others. Then I remembered my mother's death, the memory also expected and inevitable, and a dreary pang swept through me. My mother, Cassi's sister, had understood me. Had understood me so well that one morning I came home and she was dead, lying there accusingly under the crimson patch cast by the stained-glass window. I don't know if she'd planned that, or not. (My paranoia, you perceive, was that the dead were always in league against me—worse than the living. The dead, plotting to snare and to implicate, to trip and fell me and lay a naked sword across my neck.) But my mother died of natural causes, if heart attack is natural. The medical man, who like the mailman caught me in my sunglasses, and who looked at me with the same unliking, interested stare, cleared the death certificate for me disappointedly. He would, of course, have heard stories of the odd recluse duo, the mother and her daughter, living in the old colonial house under the hills. When I was sixteen or seventeen and couldn't keep out of Hammerlake town, nights, all kinds of tales were spelled out about me. The boys would whistle after my lean long flanks, nipped-in swaying waist and heavy young-girl breasts. In those days (nights) I had no wisdom at all. None. When I think how lucky I was, I tremble, even now. Caution came long after guilt, but before then it got to my mother. It made a slim artery in her heart engorge and burst. It killed her. I—killed her.

Presently the plane began to clear its throat and the fasten-up warning lights came on. I hadn't glanced about. I'd learned not to where space is confined, for this is a gregarious civilization; I too, if I could afford to be, maybe. The bug lifted on its jets and stars crowded the windows.

I don't often sleep at night, darkness has too much to offer with its silences and mysteries. But the motion and hum of the air-bug and the thick half lights gradually sent me under.

Then I started to dream. I dreamed about Easterly, which was a logical progression from the rest, the death of Cassi and my mother's death.

Easterly was the little township, sixty-two miles east

of Ares where my mother and Cassi were born, and where I grew up. My father was an ore-blaster, and when I was two years old the drill he was working on caught fire. (Catalog of death.) My mother, his widow, got the insurance payments the company awards to survivors. Aunt Cassi, an adventuress, was way off on Earth; then. My mother and I, alone without a man, became briefly wealthy.

Consciously, I can perfectly recall the copper-brick house at Easterly, on a street of copper-brick houses, for Easterly was an ore town on the boom. Asleep, I could see it in microscopic detail. Every brick shining in the sun, the neat lawn of aniseed grass running into the avenue of honeysuckle trees and the brindle oaks across the way where black-haired boys kick a ball. The mines were neatly hidden underground, but the distant towers of the three refineries gleamed and gave off tiny puffs of cotton wool. Beyond the refineries, over the river and the crescent of the dam, the meadows and the wildflowers faded into the rose-petal sands. There are ruins at Easterly. At eleven, I didn't know. One of the dry canals plunges in under the rock of an old quarry. In there.

"Come out!" my mother calls. "Bel, come out of that, it's nothing but a dirty hole. Bel, do you hear me?"

But momma, I've come to place with a tall pillar like a lily stem. Momma it's not so dark—

"Child, the sides may cave in—"

Why was I scared? I wasn't scared before. I was eleven. It was the day I started to bleed for the very first time. It was the day I found—

"Bel!"

Oh God, why am I so scared?

"Bel!"

I realized the tunnel was closing in on me after all, was dragging me away, and I beheld my mother's terrified face snatched from me, receding—

And I woke up to discover myself crying softly,

"Momma, Momma!" Like one of those dolls of centuries before.

"It's all right," somebody said. "Really it is. You're awake. It's all right, now."

I could see the air-bug, quiet, and scattered with persons who slept on without the raw edges of dreams to slash them alert again. And next to me, on the twin seat at my side, but not fastened in, a shadow saying, "Honestly, it's O.K. now," very gently, as if to the child I had been two instants before.

"Is it O.K.?" I asked, to gain time.

"Sure it is. You're back."

"Am I?"

"Truly. I swear."

He laughed, this gentle still. I hadn't looked at him beyond the first uncalculated awakening gaze that hadn't assimilated anything. But he was young. My age?

I'll have to be extra careful now.

"That's better," he said. "Look, can I get you anything?"

"Anything?" No, I must not fool around.

"Well, a brandy?"

"No thanks."

"You must have something, to prove to yourself the dream's over. I've had dreams like that sometimes."

"How do you know what kind of dream it was?"

"A bad one. Come on. Oh, I know," he said. His voice was warm, melodic. Perhaps Prokofiev had written his voice. "Last year I was on Gall Vulcan, with my brother. I freaked out on mescadrine." (Some drug.) Now he was telling me how his big brother saved him, sat and held his hand, ran him into the ground to sweat the horrors out of him, rocked him like a baby. It was extraordinary. "I'm not ashamed to tell you," said the young man in the shadow. "We shouldn't be ashamed."

"I was ashamed. Afraid, ashamed. Excited.

This was the duck-catch syndrome. I'd ducked, but

the missile had still come straight at me. In avoiding it, I'd caught the ball in my ungloved, unready hands.

"If you don't want a brandy, what about an iced fruit juice?"

I'm going to a funeral. Don't make it two.

"All right. Thank you."

He went to the auto-dispenser, and I looked at him. And when he came back and we sat drinking cold juice, I looked at him then, too. He was sunlit, even in the night cabin. He had the light bronze suntan of Novo Mars I can't even take from a ray-lamp. His eyes and his hair, like mine, were dark, and his hair was worn rather long, the recurring fashion among the young poets, the dreamers. His clothes were casual, but of good quality, and he had one of those gold ropes around his neck that are jewelers' fantasies of snakes, and have narrow graven heads and gem eyes.

"I hope you're not angry that I spoke to you," he said.

"I'm not angry."

"I have another confession." He lowered his lashes and I felt sad. Old and sad, and tired, and alone. "I was watching you when you were asleep. I was planning something to say when you woke up, but then you had the nightmare."

How rare and chill the juice tastes on my tongue, the tip of which is burning now. I always imagine it's like champagne, which I've never tasted, but how could it be?

"I wanted to talk to you, you see."

Yes. I see. I know.

I mentioned those centuries-old dolls that used to say ('Momma!') Dolls nowadays are robotic and can do anything your child programs into them. Eat, sleep, sob, dance, urinate, tell stories. And like dolls, humans, given a certain programming, will do . . . anything.

I put down my fruit juice.

"A relation of mine just died," I said flatly.

"I'm sorry."

"We were very close. It's my turn to apologize. I'm not good company right now. I want to be alone."

That was difficult to say. Laughable, but difficult.

"O.K.," he said. "Of course."

He stood up. The snake about his throat had blue eyes that comprehended me, and that glittered. But his eyes were innocent.

"My name is Sand—that's really Sand Vincent. If you need anything."

Magic formula, the exchange of names, but I only smiled at him, as stiffly and coldly as I could, and he went away.

It was so easy to make them come to me, like filings flying to a magnet. I was a lodestone. The boys on the neon-striped black candy streets of Hammerlake when I was sixteen, seventeen, seven or eight years ago. Hey, sister! Hey, baby!

There are still wolves in those damned hills!

The sound of guns, and the lights over the ridges, and the scent of burnt electric air.

I watched the cabin clock. Less than an hour to Ares. I wouldn't fall asleep again.

The Brade air-bug landed at the Cliffton Terminus Strip. Aresport has twenty-seven landing strips. Ares is a big city, though not as big as Dawson and Flamingo in the north.

Cliffton was a ghost terminus at this hour, almost deserted. However, every port had its duty-check, for drugs, for guns, for stolen goods. Machines clear the luggage, and every now and then a bag was opened. Mine got opened. The electronic eye scanned inside and hit the metal cap of the container, and an alarm went off. Aresport is too sophisticated to let a mechanism handle such matters. Two human securi-guards walked over and asked me to remove the container. Apart from the cap, it's transparent, so they looked at the red juice inside.

"Christ, lady, what's that, blood?"

Sand, having got through the check right in front of me, returned.

"Is anything wrong?"

"This lady is carrying a bottle of blood in her bag."

The guards at the port were bored and power-conscious. But here was a malign brittle good humor I could match.

"Pomegranate and tomato juice," I said. "Half a liter, concentrated, with added vitamins. My physician makes it up for me. Like to try some?"

The guards grinned. Sabella the proud beauty was turning them on, and it had been, was going to be, a long slow night on Cliffton strip.

I uncapped the jar, and they fetched plastic cups and distilled water and we mixed some and drank together. I hope they enjoyed it.

"It smells of flowers. Or hash," said Sand, perplexed.

"You want to come round the back, son," said one of the guards. "We've got confiscated Vulcan-grown hash up to the roof, no duty paid."

"And good old frecking alcohol," added the other.

"Are you going to be O.K.?" Sand asked me as we went out of the terminus building. The wide port highway strode up toward Ares. You never see the stars above a city. The revitalized atmosphere is thick, but oh the colors of their lights chalked on the under-swag of the clouds, greengage and peppermint and opal and strawberry ribs of color, as if the cities were on fire, and this their smoke.

"Yes, I'll be all right."

"Only, things seem to be happening to you, don't they?"

"Yes, they do. But it will be fine now."

"I'm not trying," said Sand, outlined against the first hour of black cloud-blazing morning city, "to be a pain in the ear. But after this—the funeral—"

"Then, I'm going home."

Say: *To my husband and my twelve babies. Say* it. Nothing comes.

Sand turned to the city.

"Pillar of fire by night," he said. He must have had Revivalist biblical training.

My heart was racing. The sight of the city was hurting me with pleasure. I have none of civilization's taint. A landscape of steel towers against hills of concrete, sings to me as does a landscape of rock pinnacles and gullies. All landscapes are one, dissimilar, yet still landscape. All one to me.

I swallowed.

"I must go now," I said. I can't even be nice to him. Dare not. "Excuse me."

I brushed by him, and a cab crawled to the walkway.

I got in and gave it directions to drive me to any middle-price hotel. (Not cheap enough to attract random fellowship, not flashy enough to attract speculation.)

Sand stood by the window.

"You won't even tell me your name?"

"I'd rather not."

"That pendant," he said.

The cab drove away.

My tongue's tip was a scald of flame.

Sunrise was at six o'clock, sunset eighteen-thirty; Aunt Cassi's funeral was set for sixteen in the afternoon. That was fortunate. The sun would already be westering behind the tall gray pines and cumulous trees and the white marble groves of the Koberman cemetery that uncle-in-law Koberman had sent me a picture of.

Why do you wear so much black, Sabella, baby?

It keeps the sun out, my parasol black. The women in the east of Earth knew that long ago. They knew other things. Anyway, what else do you wear for a Christian Revivalist burial? Black frock, black stockings, black shoes that seem to grow into the legs, as if I were born with three-inch heels. Big black hat. I am a raven. No, the ravens in the Ares Zoo are white.

I slipped the pendant inside my dress. It must have wormed out when I fell asleep on the plane and I didn't properly notice. Only Sand noticed, and perhaps the securiguards.

The hotel had been sleazier than it should have been.

On the sidewalk, between the great golden towers and the glass shards of the city, the cab whooshed through the dust. But once I was inside, the cab disowned the city, throwing it over its shoulder, racing into suburbs of grass plantings and white colonial houses.

The shadows were long and red when I reached the cemetery. There were no drivers in these autocabs to argue. I put the necessary credits in the meter and left it parked among the pines.

Westering glow, yet the sun fell on my face, my hands, like embers. I walked quickly up the path and into the chapel. The Kobermans had a Gothic twist. The Christ was white and warped and screwed by pins to his length of wood and apparently screaming. To be mercilessly nailed forever in a window; who could blame him?

There were two or three people already there, dark figures kneeling between the white bench-pews in the white light of the window. The huge jeweled cross by the lectern took your breath away. If Cassi had paid for that, Cassi had been in clover. Now she was in a box. My eyes touched the coffin in its snow drape and the nausea began as it had to. The last coffin I saw had been my mother's.

"Miss Quey, I'm so glad you were able to come. When we received no stellagram, I'm afraid I'd almost given up on you—"

The big tusker in the black formal two-piece suit spoke to me in a hushed monotone. . . . This was how you spoke in front of the dead, because they mustn't overhear the huge secret of what had happened to them. He thought I'd come to listen to the will read, shed a crocodile tear (I've never seen a crocodile), and collect, like all of them, and so he was instantly at home with me. But he introduced himself as the sender of the stella, uncle-in-law.

"You'll be coming back to the house. For the er, to settle matters."

"Yes."

He was extra pleased. He'd got a word out of me.

"And stay over, naturally. Hammerhead is quite a way."

"That's all right. I have a cab waiting to take me back to town."

"But Miss Quey—Sabella. Come on, now. You must be worn out already."

No, I'm not worn out. The sun left a line of invisible blisters all over my skin, and through the blisters my nerves were thrusting like eager wires.

The chapel had filled up, and the priest appeared in his black cassock, the lilies of death embroidered on his shawl.

Uncle-in-law wedged me into a pew. Somewhere music started and my heart stopped.

Oh Christ, let me get through this. I shouldn't be here. I'm on fire.

"*Deus,*" said the priest, authoritatively, as if he had a through line to God, "*cui proprium est misereri semper et parcere—*"

The Revivalists revived the Latin with the rest of the Revival. It's beautiful. It plays me like a harp. Everything's so bright and clear and full of pain and sorrow. Six years since I heard such words.

"*Dicit illi Jesus: Resurget frater tuus.*"

I was leaning on the pew, and weeping and I didn't really know her, and it was wrong. And it makes it worse if anyone thinks it's *right* I should be weeping.

If it goes on much longer I shall faint. They'll carry me out and the sun will smite me by day between the pine needles. It will kill me and they won't know why. They'll say I died of grief for Cassi and now I'm going to laugh.

I didn't laugh. Something made me turn, maybe the

acute instincts of the hills. And there, at the back of the chapel, his dark head bowed over his gentle mourning and the snake coiled round his throat, was Sand Vincent.

Big hog uncle took me by the arm, and guided me, guided all of us away, when it was over. At a C.R. mass you often don't see the box go in the ground. I don't know why not. Dissociation from the mortal to the spiritual things, perhaps. The way to the house lay across some open land, acres of the Koberman Ares holdings. It was a distance of half a mile, but most of them got into their cars to do it. Cars like black-sharks nosed up the road. Uncle and I walked side by side—between the tall hedges of stonework, over the lawns, the ugly house like a big pillared air-raid shelter ahead of us on the rise. Sand Vincent, head still bowed, walked about twenty yards behind us.

What should I say? I didn't at that time believe in coincidence.

"We've kept it as informal as possible. She wanted it like that. Cassilda, I mean."

Who could I think he meant? Who else had died?

"I know you saw very little of your aunt since childhood, but toward the end, you were in her thoughts."

I didn't even know what she'd died of.

"One thing," I said.

"Yes, Sabella. May I call you Sabella?"

"The man behind us."

Hog Uncle Koberman shot a glance behind us.

"Yes?"

"Is he a relation?"

"I don't know who the hell he is, Sabella. He's not with our party."

"He was in the church."

"The hell he was. Some funeral freak. Stay here, Sabella, I'll deal with it."

I stood where I was while knightly Uncle Hog went back and stopped Sand on the lawn. They exchanged words I couldn't hear, didn't try to hear. Uncle's wide back blocked out my view of Sand. I knew he'd followed me, all the way from the port. I didn't know how. I knew why.

Sand didn't try to look at me and now the exchange of words was over. Sand stood on the lawn, his thumbs in his belt, cat's paw velvet on the velvet grass. The Hog Uncle came to me with the blood dinning in his face. "That's that."

He didn't tell me what had been said. I didn't ask. Sand got smaller and smaller as we went up the slope.

Flowers wilt in too much sun. They were wilting in the hall of the air-raid shelter, petals like paper.

"You need something to eat," Hog Koberman said to me.

They were all at the buffet, like the sin-eaters of old, gobbling up the crimes of the deceased along with the paté, cakes and exotic fruit segments in silver dishes.

But I convinced him I'd eaten before I left my hotel, and I sat and watched the others. When the eaters glanced at me, they felt antagonism. Uninvolved in their activity, I was outside the pale, I had an advantage. Besides, I had refused to consume the sins of the dead. Hog Koberman introduced me to everyone, but their names slipped off the surface of my mind, and their breath smelled of sugars, proteins and digestion. They were only extras on the set.

After a while, we went into Cassi's library. One wall was book tapes, and the rest actual books, bound in leather. Long windows sliced between the stacks, and there was a globe of Novo Mars in polished rose quartz, pierced and mounted to demonstrate the axial tilt, and pierced by the sun rays, too. Even the dust was gilded by the last sun against the windows. In the middle of the oak table where we were seated was a jeroboam of wine, slightly cobwebbed from the cellar. Cassi had had human servants, who now served us with this ancient valuable drink. Cassi had really schemed things, for this was the one way you reached back from the grave, with instructions to be obeyed, rituals to be performed. I pretended to sip from my goblet.

The Hog read the will slowly and carefully. Everybody waited breathless, as if at a lottery. The prizes were big ones, and everybody got a prize.

I was last of all. Now they could observe me in turn. The sunlight lay over me in a broad shining spotlight.

"Of course, Cassilda wanted me to intimate to you, Sabella, something of the form of this bequest," said Uncle, displaying to the others, in parentheses, the reason for my mercenary attendance at the funeral. "But what it amounts to, and here I read, 'To my only niece, Sabella Quey, the entire stock investments of the Kobercor Trust, which come to her, tax paid, as the sum of eighty thousand credits.' "

The extras smiled archly. My prize was good, but not so good as the others.

The servants came around to refurbish the drinks and the Hog closed his portfolio. He drew me aside, against a blazing window.

"It may not seem a great deal, Bella, but with wise reinvestment, it could amount to a tidy sum in a year or so. How about you sign the investment procedure over to me? I'd be happy to assist any way I can."

The sun was pouring through me. I felt, maybe I looked, translucent. My skin often has that quality, but were my bones showing now? Uncle was blurred as if I stared at him through smoke. I thanked him. I'd had to keep thanking him. People like you to thank them. They do you kindnesses so you'll have to say thank you, thank you.

"And there's one other small item," said Uncle playfully.

I stood in the sun's X ray, waiting.

"Cassilda entrusted this to me, this extra small thing, to be dealt with privately. It's a little casket, and I think, well, I know, Bella, it has a very fine piece of jewelry in it, which your aunt meant you to have. Her mind was on you a lot, you know, Bel, the last days. But she wanted it secret. You know how families are,

Bel, squabbling, getting jealous. Not about the value of the token, but its sentimental worth. Now, what I want you to do. Our John Trim over there is going to go out, and I want you to slip out after him. He'll take you upstairs to Cassilda's bedroom and direct you to the casket. O.K.?"

I nodded. The Hog turned away and John, one of Cassi's servants, walked between the library doors.

As I stepped out from the sun, the room sizzled and went dark, but I moved through the darkness, after John, across the flower-garden hall. John was much older than Cassi. Had John been mentioned in the will?

The stair was mobile with white carpet over the steel. John operated the button and we rode up in silence to the third floor.

His hands on the rail, and on the bedroom's enameled handles were like parched old brown leaves. A life of sun had done that to him. Were my hands shriveling too?

"In here please, Miss Quey."

The bedroom was white silk, with bronze blinds down over the windows, hot, with that smell of too-much hygiene that supplants sickness. On the vanity table, all was laid out as if in readiness for her return, platinum-backed brushes, tetra-shell boxes; she should have been buried in here, like a pharaoh's wife, among her treasures, side by side with her long-dead spouse in the big white bed.

The casket was on a separate table. It was made of ivory, with gold on the clasps, and a gold key hanging by a ribbon.

"Excuse me, Miss Quey."

Servant John shut me in with his brown leaves, closing the doors softly.

I was supposed to open the casket, so I took the key and put in the lock, and as the lock clicked I thought, *Maybe it will explode.*

But the box didn't explode. Inside it, lying on satin, was a tiny replica of the gold jeweled crucifix I'd seen in the chapel, a lectern cross from Lilliput. It was worth about twice what she'd left me in credits.

The bedroom in the bronze blind-light was full of menace. Cassi had lain in here, propped up and guttering, and she'd plotted, and here was the result. And I didn't grasp what it was. Like death itself, the threat was invisible.

Then I saw the envelope tucked under the cross, and when I drew out the envelope my fingers were oddly desensitized, but I wondered if poison would spurt into my face when I tore the paper across.

Poison spurted. Poison pen.

I know what you are, Sabella. I didn't know until I came to God, but when I found God, He told me. His angels told me. I know what you've done. I know you killed my sister. I hope the cross cripples you, as it should. If it doesn't, I've made another arrangement. Don't try to guess what it is. You're just one of the wolves, Sabella, an animal, and animals can't guess things. Not till it's too late. But you don't have so long, Sabella. I hope it's soon, and then you'll rot, and your soul, if you have one, will writhe and shriek in Eternal Fires, Sabella, and God will let me hear you as I rest on His bosom.

I sat down on Cassi's bed and put my head between my knees, but it didn't help, and I'd known it wouldn't. So I lay back, with the letter balled in my hand, and presently I pushed it inside my frock, between my breasts where the pendant was. Next to my heart.

She'd found God, and she'd found out. Yes, that made sense. She'd had intimations, but they would seem so crazy, she'd have to go crazy before she could accept them.

When I felt a little better, I opened my purse and took out the miniature bottle of what I'd mixed up from the red juice in the container.

It's blood. We all knew it, didn't we? It's flavored with pomegranate and tomato and a synthetic grain of hashish, which acts as a preservative, and to disguise reality in the presence of securiguards. It's the blood of the deer on Hammerhead Plateau. Brought home and first stored cold with a concentrator, it thereafter keeps several days, even in my luggage.

It's going to help you, Sabella. Yes it is. Drink, it'll make you strong. In spite of the sunlight, in spite of Cassi, in spite of spite. Drink.

But the fruity odors, this time, made me gag.

I sat there shivering, feverishly turning my black straw hat between my hands. On this occasion, Sabella, it isn't going to work.

Get home, Sabella. Quick, Sabella.

Get home.

I put the cross in my purse and left the casket, and as I shut the bedroom doors, the crumpled letter stirred against my breast.

A black Pig lurked in the hall.

He'd seen me weeping in the chapel, and I must look awful now. I explained how affected I was by everything, how I wished I'd known her better. I put in a couple of lies about childhood meetings, when I was twelve or thirteen. (Cassi had visited Easterly, in the years before we moved house. I don't think she properly saw me. My mother bored her; it was duty.) But humanity loves confession and painful reminiscence. We're all bloodsuckers, one way or another. I sold my uncle on the idea that I had to go home and pull myself together and we would sign papers another day, and that was how I got free.

There were about ten minutes left of the sun as I hurried across the lawns to the pine trees. The gray shade came over me at the same instant the sun turned boiling red. I walked into the deep shadow, and threw up violently, wrenching every muscle in my body.

There was a silly little ornamental cistern nearby, for watering the lawns, recycled tap-water probably unrefined, but I rinsed my mouth and was thankful. (Do even cisterns require thanks of me?)

Then I went to the cab and leaned on it, sore and aching, too weak to get inside.

It was coming on dark. The sun had dropped while I was ill. The night was like a cool bath, even the top of the cab was cool to my hands, my forehead.

And then I heard him coming up, over the dry needles. I knew who it must be. You get to know one certain step from all others, the step of the deer, picking its path to you through the wolf-dappled night.

He put his hands on my shoulders. Gentle, gentle.

"Sabella?"

He knows my name. He must have heard the Hog using it outside the chapel.

"Sabella, are you all right? Oh, Sabella." Gently he moved me around to confront him. His handsome face was holy with its concern, eyes limpid, wanting to aid me any way he could. "You look ghastly. No. I don't mean that. You look wonderful, but you look sick." He was a saint. He was meant to be a saint. No, Sabella. He held me in his arms, tenderly, he smoothed my hair. I was trembling so much it must have been hard for him to soothe me so delicately. His skin was warm, aromatic of youth, cleanness, masculinity and desire. I could scent his life through his skin. I could scent his blood.

He eased me into the cab.

"Now, where to?"

"It has the directions," I said.

"But where? I'll pick up my transport tomorrow. I'm coming with you."

"I don't want you to come with me, Sand."

"You need someone with you."

"Not you."

"Why not me?"

My brain was going out. I was losing consciousness. He had gotten in beside me and pressed the starter, and the cab moved out between the trees onto the high road back to town.

Again he put his arm round me. I looked up against his shoulder, through his warm dark hair, into the knowing eyes of the snake at his throat.

We were at the hotel, and I didn't remember much of the journey. Sand Vincent had got my door-opener, and brought me into the room and pressed the master switch for the side lighting. Then he picked me up, (I weigh one hundred and seven, it was comparatively easy for him) and laid me down on the bed. Like a fool, I still had my sunglasses on. He took off those, and my shoes.

"You need to sleep," he said. "It's taken it out of you."

"Sand."

"Yes?"

"You've been very kind."

"I'm not leaving you," he said, "if that's what you're leading up to."

"I want—I need to be alone."

"I'll wait in the corridor, then. But that's as far as I go."

"Please, Sand. I'll call you tomorrow."

Tomorrow, I'll be in Hammerhead. Sand doesn't know my route beyond Brade. It's a big country.

Why did I leave, anyway? Would it have mattered? There are still investment papers to sign for Hog Koberman. The Hog will pursue me, grunting. Anxious to see me be a pig too, greedy for cash. No, I came here because Cassi reached out from the grave and summoned me.

"I'll wait in the corridor."

We'd been silently at work on each other all the way from the cemetery. Like two acids, smoldering each other away.

"Take the chair."

"I'll carry it into the corridor."

"No. Don't bother."

He sat down in the chair. I shut my eyes so I wouldn't see him studying me. Inside my lids, the room was empty. It wasn't Cassi that made me come here. It was I, myself.

Of course, I know now I'm going to do it. And now I know, I'm getting stronger. My pulse was beating against that scrap of Cassi's vitriol on my breast, but I could feel the second pulse, too. It was mild, lethargic at first. It was coming back from limbo, the limbo it goes to, between.

The excitement. What's it like? It's in every part of me. It's like—I don't know what it's like at this time, have nothing to compare it to, drink or drugs, or sex or religion. When I was thirteen, when I was—changing, my mother took me to Revivalist meetings. Christ had caught on in a big way in Easterly. It has been remarked, the manner in which colonies retreat to the old fashions of Earth, the clothes, the decor, the religions, as if in search of anchorage. But remarking it, it still comes fresh and sudden, new to the new planets as if they had invented it. In the new C.R. copper-brick church, momma held my hand tight, and I saw the faces of men and women burning as if the great light were about to shatter out of them, dynamite inside glass. You could almost take hold of the tension, the glorious poise on the brink of ecstasy, and then the fall.

"Sand," I said, and he started. I can lie so still I seem dead, let alone sleeping, "I'm going to take a shower."

His eyes were luminous.

"Yes," he said, and rested his head against the back of the chair.

It was altered between us. He'd ceased asking me if he could help. He sensed he could help me.

I went into the cubicle and ran the shower, and as it ran I took off my dress and undergarments and when I came to Cassi's letter, I flushed it away through the chem-flush lavatory.

I looked at myself in the jets of the shower, at my body. Sand was going to want my body very much. (Whores do it for payment, Sabella.) The pendant around my neck on the hair-thin white-metal chain was glinting, pulsing, though usually only I could see it pulse.

The sleazy hotel room was warm. I shut off the

shower and went out rain-wet, and I called his name very quietly, and Sand moved out of the chair and around and saw me. For a moment his reaction was dual, arousal and nervousness, quite normal, human: I'm beautiful, I've scared him.

I crossed to him, and slipped off his jacket. I was unsealing his shirt, quietly, quietly, and he said, "Sabella, are you certain you—" And then no more, because it was a gesture of some kind the decent human response was forcing him to make. The animal human response was already making him tremble, as I trembled when he held me before. He placed his hands at either side of my face and leaned and kissed me long and slow, and the unhuman response was beginning to well through him, what the unhuman part of me was causing to happen to him. He said my name several times as he kissed me along my throat, my shoulders, and put his mouth to my breasts. The stone lay against his cheek. (Sometimes, stretched on the wolf hills, a boy, misled by the white refracted gleam of the stone, would say to me, Is this a frecking diamond, baby?) But Sand brushed the pendant aside.

And then we were on the bed. His skin smooth and marvelous, his loins blossomed into a single hard fierce flame.

I always feel concern at this moment. Even with the basest of them, I feel a concern to make them happy. Of course, I know the reason. And I, I'd had no exquisite delight in it, not before, and not with Sand. The sensations of touch, of clasp, of physical excitement, are all for the other, the partner. Yet the prelude is sweet, being a prelude. Inside me, his rhythm was tidal. Numb to it, yet I could measure its perfection.

"Sabella—"

"Darling," I whispered, "there's something we're going to do now, something you'll like—"

"Whatever you want—whatever—"

I had the trick of this movement, being practiced. We rolled a little, and he laughed breathlessly, and then I was over him, and though we were still joined, the wonderful rhythm had broken, to allow the second rhythm to begin.

The snake shifted under my fingers, upwards two inches along his neck. His neck was strong and vital, the color of amber. I ran my tongue along the vein there, the golden vein which throbbed and spoke to me. And then I put my lips to the golden tube of the vein and kissed with the drawing kiss which bruises, brings the thing within to the surface. This was how I found the way, through this kiss, this bruising kiss, tasting the blood beneath. Sand moaned and clung to me, closing his arms around my waist, my hips, to hold me to him forever. The eye-teeth don't require great length, they are nearly long enough in most of you. They only need to be razor sharp, with points like needles, to pierce without tearing, without hurt, as the sun pierced through the globe of quartz. I pressed the flesh, the vein, with my fingers, molding it for my mouth. As I made the wound, he shuddered, and when I began to draw again with my mouth, the shudder became convulsive. I was strong, stronger than he supposed, I could retain my position with total facility, and then I must, for as the pump began, he came. And continued to come. (How could we guess, in the beginning? How could we revoke when we understood?) This orgasm, which follows the rhythm from his vein into my mouth, this climax which goes on and on, long after the fluids of it are exhausted, while this other fluid lasts, on and on and will go on until I stop drinking, or until he faints. This is what the mystery is. This is what kills.

Why does it happen in this way? I don't know. I've thought of the story that hanged men climax on the rope, the trigger of the throat, the thrust of blood into the brain and loins. Or of a surge of life whose symbol is sex, is seed, life rearing against death, for blood flowing away is the symbol of death. I've thought of the sometimes sensual pleasure of the beast giving suck. I've thought of the female spider eating her mate during intercourse. I can think. But I don't know.

And for me?

My excitement had concentrated and changed. I was no longer excited, I was beyond excitement, beyond the world. A lion crouched over its prey, you see me like that. No. It was a quite spontaneous need, like needing air to breathe. And then I was breathing air when ten minutes before I was breathing mud. I could go on, like him, different but the same, on and on. But I mustn't. I forced myself, forced myself, as if fighting against gravity.

I could picture his face. You've seen the faces of those who die in agony; did you never note that lovers look like this at the peak of joy?

I *must*, I *must*.

I raised my head.

Who told you it was messy? Great gouts and slobberings—no. A slender trickle from the one (why more than one?) minuscule wound, a thread of scarlet.

Sand's head lolled aside. He was unconscious.

I loved him, just for a minute, I loved him and I grieved for him and my pity was part of the beauty, before the shame began.

It was four hours to sunrise when Sand came to. He felt slightly dizzy, yet flooded by well-being, and hungry, as generally they did. He lay on one elbow, sometimes smiling lazily, and I fed him the steak I'd dialed for, and told him I'd already eaten my share of. My feeding him seemed quite suitable, playful and friendly, to him. Subconsciously, I believed, he understood it was his right, as prey, to be cosseted. In the light wine I'd already mixed the vitamin concentrate I'd ordered from the hotel pharmacy, along with the food. By morning, Sand Vincent would feel no more than tired. In a day or so, not even that. Unless—but I wasn't going to consider an alternative. There was a five o'clock Brade lift-off from Aresport. Mine. Even though I'd have to travel some of the route by day. I could make it now.

"That was one hell of a high," Sand said to me as we lay on the bed. "But you're one hell of a lady."

He didn't remember it all, not consciously, just that I was a good lay. In the beginning, even after I learned to control myself, to stop in time, I'd kill them because I thought they'd remember. But they wouldn't have. The truth is too absurd, it gets covered over and forgotten.

Then he put his hand to his neck and ran his fingers under the snake, and winced.

"I'm sorry," I said. "I was enjoying it, too."

He grinned. Sometimes they said, "You're a vampire!" It was a joke. You both laugh about it. But any pharmacy sells coagulant creams and healfast jel in handy purse-size packs. There wouldn't be a mark much more than a pale bruise by sunup.

"You enjoyed it too, did you," he said. He skimmed his hand across my body. He slid himself toward me, stroking, me, eager again, the way they are always eager. Then, he saw the stone. "Christ," he said, "it can't be a ruby, this size, can it?"

The pendant stone is scarlet, pulsing, warm, alive.

"Just stained crystal."

"I thought it was colorless. Why did I think that? Sabella, you're lovely."

I let him kiss me, then I eased away.

"I'd like to, Sand, but I'm so damn tired. In the morning?"

"No, beautiful. Now." And he started all over me, dreamy and stupid, with this lust the lodestone brings.

"This is to be rape then, is it?" I said. He blinked, and his face emptied. He let me go. "In the morning," I said.

"Woman, I won't let you out of this room until we do."

He fell asleep almost immediately, and in his sleep, came back to me, lying against me trustfully as a child. But the sleep was too deep for him to wake when I left him, put on my clothes and took up my piece of luggage and went away.

I paid the hotel bill through until noon next day. Sand would be ready to leave by then. He'd start at once feverishly trying to find me, obsessed by me in a way he could barely figure. But the compulsion would shrivel gradually when he didn't locate me. As long as he never saw me again, he'd be safe.

It was four years since I'd had a man. I intend the word 'had' in all its meaning—sex, con-trick, sustenance.

Four years. I'd tried to stop when my mother died. And I'd stopped. Lapsed. Stopped. Two years of lapsing, regaining ground, four years of keeping ground. But the craving never goes away. The beasts of the field appease, but I am a huntress, and my natural prey strides through the steel prairies, rides the gold mountains of the cities, the neon caves of the towns.

There are wolves on all the hills, even the hills of glass.

In the plane, as the sun was slitting the sky below and I darkened my window, I thought for the first time, *If Cassi sent me her curse and a jeweled cross she wanted to scorch me, why did she also leave me eighty thousand tax-paid credits?*

2

We moved away from Easterly because one night when I was fourteen, I went for a drive with a boy I picked up on the highway near the bearshop. It was insane instinct on my part, callousness on his. He deserved something but not what he got. The highway auto-patrol found his body in the bushes. Everybody thought he'd left his car for the usual reason, and a wildcat had attacked him, which caused a stir since Easterly isn't hunting country. He'd died of heart failure, as always. But I'd made a mess of his neck. If you allow your teeth to meet in the vein there's a hemorrhage at once. My mother waited up for me that night, and when I came home with strange hot colors on my dress, she locked us in my bedroom, and she questioned me. Six hours of questioning, but the same question, which I answered truthfully, which she would then ask me again, imploring me, mutely, to recant, to say I'd lied. We were both sobbing and shouting, and she hit me sometimes. She'd taken me to medics before, but she'd never really told them anything. The medics would prescribe for anemia. As for psychiatry, nobody reckoned it anymore, and religion, in my case, had failed. Now she had this terrible thing to face, to cope with. Her little daughter had done something momma couldn't admit, couldn't even believe, and momma still had to hide it from everyone. So she fastened on the believable aspect, that I'd been laid at fourteen and had lizards in my pants. Then, I got really sick. I started passing out, getting heat stroke after half an hour in the sun. There was a doctor who said it was photophobia, and a doctor who said it was psychosomatic. And then I killed a boy again, and the same story of wildcats went around and the men got up a shooting party, and momma and I moved west.

She'd had nobody she could confide in. Those years ate her away. The three years when it was starting in Easterly, and the four years on Hammerhead Plateau. Did I say she had no one to confide in? That wasn't strictly accurate. Sister Cassi was permanently on-planet by then, living with her husband in Ares, and him building up the Koberman Corporation. Momma must have written Cassi quite a lot. I don't think she spelled it out, the huge unbelieved terror that lowered over her days and her nights. But I suppose it was there, if you'd looked through the written lines at the howling fear behind. Cassi hadn't looked, then. Cassi had been tuned in to her man and his money, though she wrote so seldom we didn't really know about that. (She never even wrote us when he died.) Only at the end had Cassi presumably reread my mother's letters or re-dreamed them. And the angels had told her what I was, and she'd accepted their word.

The house at Easterly was isolated, twenty miles from Hammerlake, and five from the nearest flyer-halt. And it was only semi-mechanized. The ordinary mail came once a month, unless you went to town for it, but there wasn't much mail. Only registered parcels (few) and stellas (none) came to the door. The rest was left lying in the mail basket with the groceries half a mile off, where the road goes by. Hammerhead was a wild place, too. Wolves on the uplands, a dam project and dredging complex on the rim of the lake town, and bars like yellow musical boxes and those girls that somehow nobody ever properly legalized here, who still copy vamps of centuries ago, red nails, tinsel hair, winter eyes.

My mother chose the house from a catalog. Did she realize how cunning she was to choose just this house in this spot, or did she hide away the cunning, too?

There wasn't much cash left by then, enough to get

by and to add a handful of improvements, button-doors, air-conditioning, dust-eaters. (There was dust in Cassi's library. By now, dust also is fashionable again.) I got my tape deck. I'd lie on the parlor floor and listen. Prokofiev, Stravinsky, Vaeder, Nils. My music frightened my mother. It was the emanation, to her, or stimulus of my madness. She couldn't see it as balm, analgesic. She'd move to the other end of the house when I played music.

She'd try to get me to eat. I must have anorexia nervosa, now. She thought I made myself sick deliberately. I found ways to pretend, and she let herself be fooled. I'd take meals in my room, and tip them in a plastic box I kept for the purpose under the bed, and later I'd empty the box in the primitive incinerator resident behind the kitchen. School finishes on the pink planet at about thirteen or fourteen anyway, and after that you go on to mature studies at your own discretion. That could be done in the house with mailed library tapes and TV. That was safe. In the back yard, under the fifteen-foot orange tree, there was an old swing. Momma used to sit at her bedroom window and stare down at me, my nighttime insomniac swinging, swinging. When the swing was empty, she'd search the house. Often, the swing was empty.

I could run for miles on the ridges and over the star-blanched sands, among the rifts and through the fern-clotted, shade-thick canyons. I was never afraid. It was country I could comprehend, where no one knew me. Big cities are the same, you see. I learned how to hunt in the wilderness, the corridors of night, and on the things I hunted, I learned how not to kill, though it's harder with the animals, who sense the hunter from afar off, who, even when they lie down helpless in the pools of your eyes, are tensed to fly. And besides, there's no sexual communion to bind them, it has to be an act of sabotage.

One day when I was fifteen, they were repairing the road to Hammerlake Halt, and working half a mile down the slope from the house. My bedroom faced that way, and I'd looked through the blue blind, and the blued dust haze, and made out their shadows, the two men with their robot equipment. Then came this dulled-over day, sky a deep rose parasol against the sun, and I went down the road and sat on a stone, and watched. Perhaps they'd heard about a girl in the house and were keyed up to it. They turned their copper-skinned male bodies and they looked at me, and they smiled and offered me a beer.

It happens very naturally. If there are two, one is drawn more readily than the other, whichever I want the most. His name was Frank. He came back after it got dark, whistling softly, in a clean shirt. We went up into the hills, up head-on into the crushed powder of starshine. I liked him. He was thoughtful and curiously well-mannered. He told me I was Shakespeare's Juliet and I killed him and I was sorry. It was because he was the first, after so long. I couldn't stop myself. And—I liked the power over him, what happened to him, the way he clung to me.

I sat and cried, holding his hand, but his white upturned eyeballs glared like parodies of the stars.

I'd frequently heard the wolves. You can always hear them from the house. At certain seasons they fill the hills like blown sand, at others they drift away toward Brade, or westward to Montiba. But that night they were suddenly all around me, just red star clusters under the white.

I wasn't afraid of them. I didn't put it in a sentence in my head, but I understood nevertheless. They and I. Cassi had it right. One of the wolves, Sabella.

Delicate as clouds, they began to shiver down to me, and like a cloud they settled on Frank, and hid him and what they did.

Earth-imported animals don't feed on the dead. But the wolves of Novo Mars will take a fresh kill, at least from me.

The local TV news had it: Young robot-ganger savaged by wolves.

The wolves will kill, anyway. People have died

through the wolves. Periodically men stray with a weapon which doesn't fire, or in ignorance without, to meet a girl. Later, other men hunt the wolves, and the night sky leers with gun flashes.

When I was sixteen, Aunt Cassi sent me a check.

I bought some dresses and a box of face paint. I bleached my hair. I could get to town in three hours, running. I can run, a slow run, a lope, for hours. And I could look like a free-lance bar-girl. I went with the itinerants where I could, men who wouldn't be missed. We rode back in solar jeeps, in runners, in old-fashioned gas-tanked mobiles, into the wide spaces of Hammerhead. But soon I learned to take a little, only that, and then I learned the other thing, that they'd come after me for more, they'd beg me. They thought they were begging to screw me, but they were begging to die. Only three ever tracked me to the house. One beat me. He slashed me across my back and stomach, yelling. He pulled me under the orange tree and raped me and somehow I didn't touch him, and he got up roaring I was no frecking good any more, and he went away. My mother was in the house, on her knees. I'd had a toy, one of those loose-limbed things children cart around. Somehow she'd found it, and there she knelt, hugging it to her, and crying, and she said to me, "What you're doing to yourself—oh, Bel, Bel, what you're doing." But she was speaking to the toy. And not so long after, she died and fell down in the crimson blood pool of the old window. Momma. Momma.

I walked home from the Halt through the morning. I felt strong. I could take the sun because I was appeased. But around three-quarters of an hour on the road in the shining pink dusts, filed my nerves. There was a gas storm up over Smokey, the mountain that holds up the sky beyond Montiba. The gas storms start when the oxygen filler sufficiently irritates the Martian stratos, generally at the level where high lands probe the upper air. The sky veiled over a little, and claps sounded, and a big pale wind blew across my left cheek.

When I approached the house, I was bone-weary. When I'd seen the shape of it, the tall blind-sealed windows, the orange tree in a marigold of bloom, it was as if I'd been away a year. The tension went out of my sinews and I could have dropped.

I tabbed the door, but before I went in, I sat a minute on the porch on the lacework bench. The storm was building, a storm by Vaeder or Stravinsky. Dust creamed by the house, the wind made a sound like a sea, or as a sea sounds to me who has only heard it on a tape: Audio-scapes of Earth. Vol. 2. There might be rain later, Rain, but nothing else.

The guilt wasn't so bad now, because there was no need for too much guilt, and presently the gnawing, the need, would go away, as Sand's need for me would go.

I went in, and closed up, and I was really secure at last.

My bed is a copy of an old four-poster. Carved doves and pineapples decorate these posts, and navy gauzes hang down. There is only space else in the room for the vanity table blocking the window with its litter and its mirror. I can see myself in mirrors. The idea that I might not comes from the same myth that says vampires cast no shadow. Shadow and mirror image are both primitive ciphers for the soul. The myth implies a vampire has no soul. Maybe I haven't, but I've met others who surely haven't too. We all cast shadows, we all show in glass.

On the other plaster wall, where I could see it through the gauze, was the picture.

It was the reproduction of a holy picture, painted by a medieval artist in the days when there was only one world, and they thought it was flat. It depicts Mara, the mother of Christ. Her name means bitterness. But God is telling her she is going to conceive immaculately, and the artist has used the then popular symbol of the pencil-thin ray of light piercing the crystal goblet in her hands—piercing but not breaking. The analogy is flawless and beautiful. Her head's tilted back and she's so happy, so exalted, but it won't last. Mara-bitter. Her child will suffer. A mother always takes it hard.

I woke in the initial blush of night. The storm was over. The utter stillness of the wilderness hung like a velvet canopy on the house, the land.

I had a vague cramp in my stomach, but that was nothing, and would pass. But as I lay there in the deep dark, I could see starlight through the blinds, licking the oddments on the vanity table. And I recalled it was Cassi's birthday check that bought me my disguise as a bar-girl. Then I wondered about the credits again, but pushed them mentally aside, because she'd gone crazy, and that was why she'd threatened with one hand, gifted with the other.

And then I wondered about the town, the neons, and the boys who called after me, and the way my tongue burned as if a drop of flame were on the tip of it. I thought of how I had them. How I drank them. Breathed them. I thought of Sand.

I got up and shivered, and went downstairs in antique Earth-model jeans and shirt. Perhaps I'll go out tonight. Perhaps the deer are running, Montiba way, where the corrals lie like supper tables on the rouge-black rocky meadows.

I got some real orange juice from the freezer and put it through the thaw box and drank it. I took a cigarette from the carton. They had each a couple of grains of the synthetic hash you can buy at any druggist's. I smoked, and the cramp dulled in my belly.

My coffee-black hair showed natural highlights like pale brass reflecting in the windows. Remember when it was acid-drop blonde, Sabella?

The stone glittered between my breasts. It was only rosewater then, pallid, dying, the rich scarlet sunk away. Faithful barometer. Once it was always red, sometimes so red it was a coal, a wolf's eye.

I put a tone poem by Nils on the music deck.

I shut my eyes, and saw myself alone in this house for sixty years.

I waited till the Nils was done, then switched off the deck. I crossed the hall and buttoned open the door and stepped out on the porch.

And as I stood there, facing down the slope toward the road, I saw a pinprick of light ghosting along the road's surface, coming from the east, from Hammerlake.

Traffic goes by on that road at night, not often, now and then. But this car came level with the dirt track that swivels up from the road, and the car swiveled with it. The car was coming for me.

The headlight threw a blank page of light across the house and went out. The car parked about forty yards away where the road flickers back into scrub grass.

It was my uncle, the Hog. He wanted me to sign his goddamn papers.

The car door lifted. Someone got out, the door closed.

Somewhere, there was a whisper of cicadas.

He was poised in the darkness with only starlight to see by.

It was Sand.

"Here I am," he said. He said it not boldly but with shyness. A bag hung from his hand. "I had to see you again, Bella. I didn't believe it when I woke up and you'd gone. Why did you? Sabella?"

"How did you find me?" I said, having to say something.

The cicadas, who rarely speak around the Plateau, intimidated by our larger voices, had crushed themselves again to silence.

"It's so simple to find anyone you really want to."

The Hog knew where I was, maybe others of Cassi's circle. Sand had followed me to Cassi's house before. Maybe Sand had paid the servants a visit and just been plausible enough to elicit information.

I want you, baby, said the night with a hundred voices (So many? Less? More?) the men who had returned for me. Not twenty yards away, a man had torn into me under the orange tree. Why hadn't I killed *him*? He had earned it.

"Sand," I said. My voice was husky.

Sand, I don't want you. You make me sick. I hate your body and the way you lay me and Sand—and Sand—

"Bella," he said. His voice was one caress. He made my name magic.

"I don't want you here."

"Yes you do. You do want me. Maybe we both should be honest, for once. But then, it goes beyond honesty, Sabella."

He dropped his bag and came to me and grasped me against him, and he was breathing as if he'd swum for shore from some treacherous river, and I was the shore, and now he was home, he was safe.

"Don't cry, Sabella. Why are you crying?"

"I don't want you."

But I was pulling at his arm. We were actually scrambling over the porch, into the house.

The door was still open. The night leans on the door, staring.

Sand pinned me against the wall.

Flesh was grass.

He couldn't wait for me. He didn't know he would react quite like that. He apologized even as he ripped my shirt.

Centuries ago, men dying of tuberculosis, were discovered to have a high sexual drive.

Incubus and succubus imparted such exquisite pleasure to their victims during intercourse that the victims could not resist them, shunning their human partners for the embrace of death.

Be patient. Don't kill him.

You will, but not yet.

He won't come back, of course. Another myth, vampiric resurrection. He won't rise from the grave. He'll lie in it. And all his amber and bronze and sable will combine to form decay.

He cried out, and then the whirlpool choked him and swept him under. He only thought he'd escaped the river.

And I breathe again.

We had three nights, two days between, some hours more. All the while I wanted to baby him, care for him. Don't turn away. *Quid est veritas?* This is mine. All the time I was killing him I wanted him to live. I wanted to help him. Perhaps others do this. Kill each other, but always wanting to restore. But he was a drug to me, I to him. Of the two, he was the more importunate. He didn't know for a long while, almost to the last, what I was doing to him. Sometimes they never knew.

We didn't go out of the house. We—he—made love. And I used his lovemaking. I fixed him meals, after I'd dialed groceries from town. My mother taught me to cook. I cook well. I gave him steaks and wholewheat bread, green vegetables, red fruits, clear wines like morning. I pumped vitamins into him. He wasn't truly weak until the ultimate night.

You're thinking of the farmer who fattens his pig for the kill.

Did you ever eat the pig?

It's love that made me preserve. Guilt, despair.

He talked a lot about his brother. That was the subconscious again. It became apparent from his dialogues concerning this man, his brother, that Sand had been rescued by him many times. Not only from the mescadrine trip on Gall Vulcan, but from petty crimes years before, a dangerous liaison or two, debts. Sand was born a victim. I say this not to excuse myself, for it does not excuse me. But he'd traveled twisting ways, and snares had molded to him. Sand was a prophetic name. Sand that blows and forms many configurations, that can never settle, that is a mere residue of rock. Then I began to wonder if his mind was clouding, if he were hallucinating, for Sand's brother became a massive figure on the skyline of everything Sand said, an angel with blazing wings. Was it that the subconscious, anxious to provide another rescue for Sand in this extreme cul-de-sac, kept supplying the illusion of a brother? Possibly, the brother was not real and had never been.

The second morning, the mailman came. I'd forgotten about mail. He brought the registered packet which contained my certificate of holdings and my uncle's drawn-up documents whereby I could sign the investment paraphernalia over to him. The Hog was taking a fee, naturally. His letter assured me he had to, to see things legal. But I looked at all this days later.

The mailman, who again required my thumbprint, stared at my wrapper, and in the lenses of my black glasses.

"Sorry to wake you, Miss Quey."

He pivoted against the fragile sky, gazing long and hard, at Sand's car parked on the scrub grass by the track.

"Long time since I seen one of them. Ares I.D. digit panel."

He went on gazing. I held the packet in my hand.

There's menace here. He means me to feel menaced. But what can he do, what is he insinuating he can do?

"Visitor?" he said to me.

I could keep quiet, which might goad him further, though to what?

"Yes."

"You don't get so many of those."

"Thank you," I said.

"Thank you," he repeated automatically. "That's a nice car. Old model. Self-drive or auto. Nice."

"Thank you."

"Some morning," he said, "I'm going to buzz this door and you're going to come out with your clothes on."

I buttoned the door shut, but he went on grinning at me through the smoked glass. I walked away before he did, and his grin was focused on my spine as I passed through the blood splash of the big window.

Sand was lying on one elbow, reading, among the cushions on the bed. The house was cool and sweet with the air-conditioning. The blinded room was blue, and Sand's body and hair filtered blue. Even his eyes, the pages of the paper book.

He glanced up and he smiled at me. "She walks in beauty like the night," he said, "and all that's best of dark and bright, meet in her aspect and her eyes."

I sat beside him, and he let go the book, and laid his head in my lap and looked up at me.

"I've never felt like this before. And I've known some trips."

"How do you feel, Sand?"

"Floating. And as if," he smiled once more, pondering, "as if I'm a pane of window glass. What are we on, Sabella?" I didn't answer and he didn't seem to need the answer, and next he said, "Last time we made it, did I black out? I think I did for a moment. But it was wonderful, Sabella. As good for you?"

"Yes."

"I keep thinking," he said, "I *haven't* been honest with you. Jace—did I tell you about him?" Jace was the big invented brother. "Yes, I did. Did I tell you about my father? My father was incredible. Daniel. He was like being alive. He was so full of life, he was like —some kind of sun. And he was crazy. I loved that man. And Jace, he's like that man all over. . . ." He fell asleep, and the fiery jewel, swinging above him, reflected on his cheek, which now was hollow.

A little after sunset, he wanted me. I tried not to take anything from him, but he dragged my mouth to his neck. *Dragged* me. It isn't the same without, you understand, not after it's begun. Finally, I am as incapable of resisting as he.

After midnight, he started to die.

He wasn't scared. He was floating, as he'd put it. The heart gets lethargic, its sluggishness compounded by the loss of blood. I'd seen it happen quickly, in a single night, or less. But with Sand, I'd had the chance to preserve him, keep him alive. I'd never had that chance before. To watch it happen, slow, then steady and sure, like light going from the sky.

He had opened his eyes as far as they would open, which was only now a third of the way, the pried lids like heavy shutters. But at his neck the snake was still alert. Those watching, knowing, unsensual eyes would never close.

I could kill him now, simple as turning out a lamp. We didn't need to couple. His body had learned the connected responses. If I took from him now, he'd spasm anyway, and die in bliss, not guessing.

He seemed to love to say my name, a thing I'd noticed with the others.

"Sabella," he murmured, holding my hand, "Sabella—Bella—Bella."

After Frank, I'd tried to cut my wrists. I say tried. I couldn't do it. When your whole process is geared to survival, as in the hunter it has to be, calculated suicide is as hard to accomplish as to kill in cold blood would be for someone else.

Sand was young, and he had been strong. It was so stupid to realize that transfusions, cardiac assist, rest and sedation, could save this life which was trickling steadily out of him. Seventeen miles away, this side of Hammerlake, there was a hospital. It sat on a rise among palm trees, a hideous white cube that saved lives. It would be straightforward. Sand's car with its auto-drive on the night-clear road, could cover the ground in less than ten minutes. Next, I'd leave the car and Sand in it, hit the emergency button on the hospital gate, and run. Who could run better than Sabella?

Oblivion might cure him of his obsession. If he came after me again. I could go up into the hills. The longer he was away from me, the easier it would be for him. For him.

But there wasn't much time.

I broke the plasti-cover on two of the vitamin shot dermics and pumped the goodness through his pores. At the same instant I was smoothing the heal-fast jel over his throat. At the touch, he roused.

"Sabella," he said drowsily, "have you been drinking my blood?"

O.K. To a medic bending over him: "I met a lady who sucked my blood." The medic wouldn't believe him.

"Darling," I said, "we're going for a drive."

"Sure," he said, smiling. I helped him to sit up, and I dressed him as best I could. He had no more stamina now than the floppy doll my mother had held to her, kneeling on the floor. "I don't mind" he said. "Eternal life. Beautiful Sabella."

I carried him down the stairs. I'm unusually strong, but it was awkward.

"Why, Sabella," he marveled dreamily, "You're carrying me. Jace used to carry me," he said, "but Jace is built like a gladiator."

I got him through the door, over the porch. I opened the car, and managed to angle him onto the rear seat. Not every car has a rear seat. It was lucky Sand's car was a throwback model.

"Sabella," he said, "there's something I have to tell you."

"Later, Sand. There'll be lots of time later."

I got in and shut the car. I switched on the auto and keyed in the directions. The car revved itself, exploding the framework of the night.

"I'm cold," he said.

Miserere mei, Domine . . . conturbata sunt omnia ossa mea. . . .

Forgive me, God. Let him live. Let me be quick enough.

Sabella, you're insane.

The car spun itself around, and flared down the track toward the road, going so swiftly you scarcely felt the bumps.

"Where are you, Sabella?"

"I'm here, honey."

"If I tell you something about myself, don't start hating me."

"There's nothing to hate."

"Please don't hate me. Your aunt Cassilda Koberman—right? She had a guy who worked for her, an old guy, a servant, John Trim."

"Sand, don't talk."

"You don't know what I'm going to say."

"That he told you how to find me, because Cassi knew."

"Not—not quite. Christ, I'm cold, Sabella. I feel terrible, Sabella."

Horror fills me. If I'd let him die in the house he'd have died without pain.

"It'll be better soon," I said. It will. It will.

I could hear him shivering then, his teeth chattering as he pushed the phrases out. We were on the concrete road, racing east to Hammerlake. The speedometer showed one hundred and forty.

"I kept wanting to tell you, Bella. Once I understood how wrong they were, and how I—felt about you."

"Hush."

"No, listen—Cassilda Koberman was your enemy. She left you a handful of credits in her will, like bait, to draw you out of hiding. Then she primed old Trim with stories about you. She never told him what it was you were supposed to have done, but she implied plenty. The death of your mother was suspicious, you were a whore—old John Trim got the notion he was meant to hunt you down, bring you to justice. They both had this godawful Revivalist thing. She left him a stack of cash, privately, the way she left it to her bloody church. I told that fat man at the cemetery that I was a relation of Trim, but Trim had hired me to get friendly with you, to suss you out. Can you hear me, Bella? I've run a little private investigation agency in Dawson for about a year. Business was poor till this stunt came up. You see, Bella, that's how I was on the plane to Ares. I was watching for you, and the check-out tipped me when your name came through the machine. That's how I always knew where you'd be: the funeral, Cassilda's house. I even found you here on Hammerhead. But that wasn't—I knew straight off on the plane it wasn't my job any more, that they had it wrong." He stopped, gasping for breath. Then he said, "Am I dying? What have you done to me?"

The car streamed over the concrete, speedometer at one hundred and fifty-one, maximum.

I remembered the Hog marching to Sand across the lawns, returning to me with a congested face, boasting no triumph. I remembered John Trim's frail brown leaf hands shutting me in with Cassi's casket of bane.

I had to make a decision. This is the nearest to the abyss I've ever been. I ought to let him die.

But I can't.

And then the road bent into a tunnel of rock, and as the dark of the tunnel clambered over the car, I saw something beyond the tunnel about a hundred yards along the road. I slammed the brake button, and the car threw itself to a halt three feet from the tunnel's end. And in the dark I sat and stared out through the windscreen at a bar of light dividing the road, and the bright gems of neon that spelled the words RANDOM ROADBLOCK.

Sand asked me if I was angry, and if that was why I'd stopped the car. Then he asked where we were going. He seemed to have forgotten what he'd said previously, he seemed to assume he had a virus, influenza, something like that. Then he told me his father, Daniel, had never had influenza and then he asked me when Jace would arrive.

All during this, I was looking at the roadblock sign, and the barrier across the road. Such checks on traffic across the deserts are irregular but thorough, carried out on suspicion, or just precaution to see what's going where, and when, and why, and with what cargo. They'd search the car and ask questions about Sand, the state he was in. And who was I and what was my involvement. I'd taken chances in my adolescence, chances that made me shake when I recalled them, and I'd been fortunate. (Oh I don't mean the law would react to what I was. But pervert, murderess, to all of that.) And now trouble was on every side of me, on every side one slip and the precipice yawned.

I said, I'm geared toward survival. I was like someone with half vision, and what I could see was my own life, and just a blur by it that was the life of Sand.

I grasped quite suddenly what I had to do.

I opened the car door.

"Sand, it's just a little way. Will you help me? It won't be for long."

I carried him back down the rock tunnel out into the night on the other side, the way we'd come a minute ago. I laid him in the still-warm dust just out of sight of the road. The night-morning was black, cool, not cold. The stars were friendly above. He was out, all the time I carried him. But he was breathing, shallowly. I took off my jacket and spread it over him.

"I won't be long, baby."

I ran back to the car. I jammed the auto button with the self-drive, the thing they say idiots often do. It was dim in the tunnel, but I scooped up the dust and smeared the digit panel. Maybe they wouldn't bother to check it, anyway, if they checked the car and it wasn't packed with anything illegal.

I walked out of the tunnel and straight toward the roadblock and into the light.

There were three automatic electric flash-guns set half charge on the barrier. Two men in the uniform of the Hammerhead road patrol sprawled on the roadside bank with a bottle and a box playing out softly live news, weather, and slow-beat music from the Montiba Smokey Impulse Tower. Both men got to their feet.

"You know," I said as I came up, "God and his angels must have sent you to me."

The men grinned.

"What's the problem?"

"I've jammed my damn car button again. And there isn't a fixit place for thirty miles."

"Oh, we can fix it, lady," said one of the men. "But I'll have to check your car, too."

I saw the roadblock for the first time.

"You after me again? What did I do this time?"

"Not you, lady. At least, I hope not you."

They offered me a drink from their bottle and even a plasti-cup to go with it, but I explained I was desperate to get to Canyon where my man would experience apoplexy when I told him about the car buttons.

Still grinning, but with one of the auto guns unlinked from the barrier and trundling after to cover me, the bigger man strolled with me into the tunnel. He didn't check the digit panel, just the seats, the seat storage and the rear compartment. He did it all humorously, showing his powers of search but not supposing they were necessary. He untangled the jam on the dash with a device from his pocket. He told me where I could buy such a device in Hammerlake. Then he extracted a pack of cigarettes. He demonstrated no wish to leave me. I thought of Sand beyond the tunnel, his strained heart struggling through each pulse.

"You know," said the patrol man, "you're kind of nice looking."

"Am I?"

"I'd say you were. I'd say you might be nice all over."

"Hey," I said, "do you have something to write with?"

Once we got over the double entendre of this, I gave him an invented call number.

"Any time after ten. If a man answers, say you're the Hammerhead police. That'll knock the oxygen out of him."

He might never take me up on this anyway, the boredom of the roadblock being over. If he did, either he'd get the unlisted tone, or a surprise.

He said I could drive on now, they'd open the block up for me to go through, and he walked away out of the tunnel. As soon as he was twenty yards down the concrete, I turned and ran in the other direction. My plan was to bring Sand back to the car just as I'd unloaded him, in the tunnel's cover, lay him on the floor and drive straight through the block. They wouldn't flag me down again, and if they did, they wouldn't check the car.

I reached the tunnel and crossed to the dust-floor, and Sand wasn't there any longer.

My jacket was, but nothing else. Only the scuffed dust, and a slur that might have been a footprint, before the patchy shrubs took over.

I'd been with the patrolmen about ten minutes. Sand had been comatose. But presumably the air had brought him to. Either he'd panicked, or he had just started moving automatically, to find me, or someone. Maybe he was looking for Daniel or for Jace. Maybe he hurt too much to lie quiet. But he hadn't the strength to go far.

I called him, softly. I didn't want the men by the block to hear me. In any case, I only had a few minutes at most before one of them came back into the tunnel to see why I hadn't driven on out.

The wind blew like a lake's ripples across and across the wilderness. I picked up the jacket and put it on.

I went out over the plain, one way, now another. Even in the dark the stars were bright and there the land was almost flat, apart from the ridge that ran down to form the tunnel. Sand couldn't have climbed that ridge, but he could have wandered among the shrubs, the slender, dryly flowering clumps of trees. A parched watercourse, long abandoned, was cut like a scar in the soil. I stared into and along it, because he could have fallen there. But it wasn't there that he fell.

The road was two hundred, two hundred and thirty yards away. I could see the flush of the roadblock's light beyond the arched shapes of the ridge and the tunnel. They must have been going into the tunnel by then. It was too late. I couldn't get back to the car, even when I found Sand.

Then I found him. Of course, then.

He'd come quite a way, as if there were really something out there on that flat easel of earth and night that he had to get to. The wind stroked his hair as he lay there on his face. He was dead. I could have saved him, even with the roadblock, I could have, if he'd waited.

"Why didn't you wait for me," I said to him and I crouched by him, as if for an answer. One of his cheeks was pressed in the dust, the other half turned upward, and luminous, or so it seemed, and the lid of the eye was luminous as if the eye shone through, looking at me. Somehow the snake rope had twisted so that its eyes could look at me too. The dead are always in league against me.

Naturally, the men would have reentered the tunnel then, found the empty car. They'd search for me, then or the next day. They'd stumble on Sand. They'd think that strange, a magic trick, a girl into boy. The digit panel of the car is an Ares registration. A call to Ares could tell them who bought or hired the car. Then they would trace Sand to John Trim and discover who Trim wanted investigated and it was me. Then they'd remember the girl on the road was like Trim's description of Sabella Quey.

It didn't matter what they could tie on to me, or can't. One connection with one of these deaths, these men who die in the darkness, one connection could trigger others. Easterly. The wolves. A spark spinning along a fuse. But not without evidence.

I gathered Sand up in my arms. It was harder, much harder since I had to run with him.

Back there in the tunnel, I heard Sand's car cough as someone manually revved the engine.

Run, Sabella. And Sabella ran.

The incinerator came with the house. It was fashionably antiquated but functional, a five-foot square black drum with a chemical filter chimney that odorlessly smoldered day and night in my mother's time, that didn't often smoke in mine. But it had been at work the past day or so, because Sand had been with me. Leftovers, cartons, wrapping, the incinerator had been busy. The press-button chute was large enough to take an item a whole four feet around. Back before my mother and me, the chute had obviously had to serve larger objects than are common to domestica. And now. Now it had to serve a man.

It had been four hours, going home, carrying Sand. I'd had to lower him to the ground many times. Gradually he ceased to be handsome, pitiful and important. He became a sack of beans I had to haul, my penance, unhuman. I moved a mile or so off the road, because one of the patrolmen was sure to come looking for me or radio for others. As I staggered the last steps toward the house, the brink of the sky was rinsing itself colorless ready for sunrise.

I bore him to the chute. I pushed the igniter to feed the flame inside, and sat down while the furnace heated. I held him in my lap, and we were the Pietà.

Then, when the furnace was ready, I fed him in, let the outer door close, and heard the inner door open and the flames rush up as he dove through into them.

So callously she burned his body, the evidence which might condemn her.

There is no way I can prove it wasn't like that. If you held a knife, would you stick it in your heart, or would you throw it away? Sand had become a knife. But, no. The knife is also your child.

The smoke from the chimney was blue, and the sun came up in it.

The heat from the proofed incinerator was slight, but greater than I had ever known it, even in my adolescence, when my mother burned her old dresses from Easterly, and those albums she and my father had kept together, stills of their wedding and their two anniversaries and my birth. We all go up in flames.

I'm cold, Sabella.

Not anymore, my love.

The ash and melted residue was shunted away beneath into an underground pit. Here it slowly amalgamated with the soil, and if you dug down at the farther opening of the pit, ten feet from the kitchen door, there was an ashy compost. But we had never needed it.

I'm not leaving you, Sabella.

The jewel between my breasts, catching the sun, was the color of a dying rose.

Five days later, I walked down to the delivery box at the edge of the road.

I'd heard nothing. No one had come to the house. I'd been listening to all the news bulletins as I hadn't done for years. But even the local news from Smokey Tower hadn't carried word of a ghost-girl and a car, or a young man who'd been out this way and vanished. It had occurred to me that perhaps Sand had informed no one that he was following me to my very doorstep; that possibly the car dealer in Ares had mislaid Sand's name. Snatches of Sand's reveries came back to me. Possibly not everything was true, or legal. Possibly they'd never trace him through to me anyway. I'd remembered the mailman by then, who'd seen Sand's car parked at the end of the track. But if he'd been sure of a search or of his facts presumably by now he would have spoken out. His manner had registered as sly, a personal antagonism. When he came again, I'd know. As for the Hog, Sand had told him he was related to Trim. And in fact, the only definite potentially damning link between Sand and myself, was Cassi's servant, John. And again, his personal and suppressed form of malice might hold him silent and stultified.

There was a letter in the box, an unregistered letter.

When I opened it, I saw it was from the Hog. There was some grist about having sent me the papers I should sign if I wanted him to deal with my credits. There was a pompously sentimental footnote. He knew I'd be very sorry to hear that John Trim, Cassilda's manservant, had suffered a fatal stroke on the second night after the funeral.

I sat on the ground and read these sentences over. I think I laughed a little. Because, for once, the dead had aided me.

Perhaps it was the shock of seeing the whore-murderess in person that killed John. He had seemed remote, disinterested, in my vicinity, it must have cost him dear, boiling underneath for vengeance, justice. He was older than Cassi, he had looked ephemeral. Revenge had been too big a legacy to leave him.

Cassi, you failed. The prime agent is removed from the stage. And Sand—

My pendant is clear white, Sand. And all night the pain in my belly comes at me like the wolves. I'm living on diluted concentrates and the blood of fruits.

Your metal and your silk are cinders, trash.

And if you lay here dead, right now, I'd burn you again.

The tenth night I hunted, on the hills. The wolves were singing like broken silver saws.

The next night, I went to Angel Meadow, north of Hammerlake, the cemetery where my mother is buried.

Cassi didn't come to my mother's funeral. Nobody came but me, though curiously enough someone else was being buried at precisely the same hour in a neighboring plot, with a somber crowd, and an incredible importation of horses and carriages, emanations of that earlier world the colony planets cling to. It wasn't, in either case, a Revivalist burial. In theirs show took the place of religion. Soil rained on the coffin, and white flowers rained on it, and women desperately rained tears. Twenty paces off, the polished horses stamped. I'd never seen a horse before, certainly not with plumes. There were torches, too, though why these people also needed the night for their burying, I didn't know.

I hadn't cried over my mother's grave, though I cried in Cassi's chapel. Maybe my tears are the sweat of my calumny, and I had not yet learned I was utterly to blame for everything. I was eighteen. I was still blonde.

Obviously the gates were long shut that midnight when I revisited, but the wall was accessible. The cross leaned a fraction over her gray bed. I had never brought her flowers. I didn't pray or stupidly, humanly, attempt to speak to her; I just sat there on the turf, and I could smell aniseed grass, somewhere, like the lawn at Easterly.

When I came back over the wall, and started home, I had the urge to look behind me several times. There was never anyone there, and I think I imagined it. The pursuit had not yet begun.

Part

TWO

The Avenger

1

Two months after the smoke from the incinerator faded, a new mailman called at the house.

It was noon, the light hitting the walls like a frozen explosion, the tinted reflections of the blinds stamped in a patchwork on the floor. I'd been on the hills that night, and though I wasn't sleeping, I was lying on the parlor sofa with the music deck playing, when the buzzer from the porch drilled through. The Hammerhead mail might be delivered any time of day, for traditionally service to the Plateau wilderness is constant but erratic. But the buzz was like voltage going through me, for a moment, before my nerves dimmed down. For I was about to find out if this other enemy of mine remembered Sand's car parked on the track.

Yet, when I went to the door, even through the smoked glass, I could see it wasn't who I anticipated.

I opened the door, and he turned around slowly, like some big animal turning at a noise it doesn't fear.

"Mail," he said in a flat friendly drawl. He held a square package in one hand.

Behind him, pink noon heat shimmered, land and sky flowed over into each other. He stood out on the glare as if drawn on it and then blocked in with rich heavy color. He was six feet two. His skin was tanned like a brown-gold wood, and with the same sheened finish to it. His hair was black, and his pants and his shirt were black, and he wore black lenses over his eyes just as I did. It was as if we had both dressed in the same uniform in order to contend in some duel, in which, perhaps, sunglasses would actually become weapons.

Certainly, he wasn't wearing the uniform of the mail service.

"A very fancy order, lady," he said. "All the way from Flamingo." And he grinned. His teeth were beautiful, as if he had filled his mouth with winter snow.

"I didn't order anything from Flamingo."

He lifted the box. Black hair on hands and forearms and chest: each hair neatly done as if each were painted on with a fine brush and coal-black ink.

"Miss Ritter," he said.

"No. I'm afraid you have a wrong address," I said.

"It says here, Miss Ritter. You're Miss Ritter?"

"No."

"You have to be Miss Ritter."

The heavy colors of him, the heat that seemed to focus through him from the sun beyond, were becoming oppressive, almost frightening.

"Print here, please, Miss Ritter."

Like a scent, I could smell that strange odor which an intelligence gives off, a biting, honed intelligence, playing dumb.

"My name isn't Ritter."

Again he smiled. He invited me.

"What *is* your name then, lady?"

"My name is Quey."

"K-A-Y."

"Q-U-E-Y."

"Qwee?"

"Quey."

"O.K. Hannah Qway."

"Quey. Sabella Quey."

"That's sure a pretty name," he said. "Sabella. Still think this package is for you. Maybe you go in for made-up names."

I put my hand toward the door button. I can move quickly. He moved quicker. He was in the doorway, and the door wouldn't close on him. He didn't come into the hall, he stayed in the doorway. He looked immovable, in or out. He held out the package.

"Why don't you open it, Miss Qway?"

"It isn't for me."

"Look at the label and make sure."

"I don't need to look at the label."

"Ah, please."

So I glanced at the package. It had no label on at all.

"There's no label."

"Maybe there is, and you just can't see it."

I was afraid of him. Why? I'd met the pushy kind. I'd handled them. Handled some into the earth. My voice didn't show my fear.

"I can see there's no label."

"If you took off your sunglasses," he said, trying to help me, "maybe you'd see better."

"Get out," I said.

My heart hit my throat twice every second.

Then he took off his own dark glasses, and raised his head, smiling, and the glow of the stained-glass window revealed to me his eyes. They were like mahogany, but they shone. The black lashes were thick, almost coarse in their thickness. And because he was laughing at me, the outer corners of the eyes were scarred with hair-thin silver cracks in the gold.

"Ever play the imitation game, Miss Qwee?" he asked me. "I do it, and now you do it."

"You're not with the mail service."

"Then you'd better call the police."

The long silence filled the hall. The glare streaming around the edges of him was a crucifixion.

"What do I have to do," I said, "to make you get out. You want money?"

"It's true what the man said."

A pause. He continued to smile at me.

"He said you never answer the door with your clothes on."

I was not in my wrapper, but in a floor-length black smock, with an ornamental button-up, the top four buttons of which were undone.

"How about jewelry," he said, and I know he'd seen the glint of the pendant.

"What you're looking at is glass. You'd get twenty credits for it. There's nothing else."

"There's you."

When he said that, a constriction of terror came up through me. We know I'm not innocent. We know for me it's as if they comb my hair, rough or tender, no more than that. So why terror?

He'd been fraternizing with the mailman. He had a box he wanted me to open. I took it abruptly from his hands, ripped off the plasti-cover and the card reinforcer. One side of the interior gives, and something drops out onto the wooden floor with a clack.

It was the ivory casket, closed by its gold lock as when I had first seen it, and the key on the ribbon, the casket Cassi's heirloom had been in, and her poison-pen letter. I'd left it behind in the house at Ares. Now this man, who was eight inches taller than me and weighed around seventy pounds more, had brought the casket to my door. (Sabella, his height and weight don't matter. You aren't scared of those. What looms so great is the look on his face, in his eyes, that sense of a coiled spring. A thousand yards of coil ready to unwind like a whiplash.)

"You say this came from Flamingo." I sounded calm. I sounded indifferent. He knew I wasn't, but the control might throw him a little, not that he'd show that anymore than I was showing my own emotions.

"Flamingo? Did I say that? Ares."

"Who gave it to you to give to me?"

"Who gave it to me to give to you? The mail service, ma'am."

Now he was abruptly the simple dumbbell again; the dope, worried about his job, worried that I might misunderstand. I stood ossified, and he said, "My buddy is sick, ma'am. Something he ate. So I offered to bring this package out to your house. He couldn't make it, ma'am. He was puking. Real bad puking. Puking to left of him, ma'am. Puking to right of him. Volley and thunder . . . ma'am."

The mailman had gabbled about me. This one, this

new enemy, intrigued, had persuaded or coerced the other into letting him bring me my package instead. Could it be that straightforward? Did they really gamble that I was so deep into shady dealings that I wouldn't complain? And why no label on the package, which seemed to have been opened and resealed. And why the ploy with a false name and an erroneous city, as if I must declare myself and my connections. There was no letter in with the casket.

"Just need your thumbprint now," he softly reminded me. Soft, his voice was almost a mumble, lazy, a beast purring.

But he *didn't* have the nail block for prints. Instead he extended his hand to me, well-formed, hirsute, with its sinews of fire under the skin. The gesture was another invitation. Then suddenly he grabbed my fingers into his. His hand was hot and dry like the desert in the sun.

He wrung my fist into a knot, as if he meant to break the bones, and all the while he went on smiling. But his eyes, were cold. I couldn't tell if he was merely a sadist, if he was enjoying this. No, it wasn't that. There was more. Only I couldn't read it.

Then he let me go. He saluted me and sauntered out onto the porch. I walked slowly to the door button. I'd learned, for he'd already taught me, that he could be swift enough to negate that action if he wanted. At the top step, he paused.

"While I'm on the premises," he said, "maybe you can help me. I'm making inquires, you see, Miss Kerway. About my brother."

I didn't even blink. But then I hung by a thread.

"Could there possibly be two of you?"

He laughed. He made a meal of laughing. He rocked around and clapped his hard palm against the porch rail. He knew I wouldn't close the door.

"Nice, Miss Ker-woo. Nice, Well, Miss Ker-wuk, I'm looking for my kid brother, Sand. Sand Vincent. I guess you never heard of him."

Falling.

"I guess I never did."

"Your loss, Miss Ker-wak. Your loss." He swung down the steps. There was no car visible, not even on the road below, where the genuine mailman parks. When he turned once more, he had his sunglasses on again. "See you," he said, "Jezebella."

Why can't I take the sun, even the rays of a health-lamp? No, it's no part of a myth. The sun harms me. I think it's my blood. My blood is built of blood, purer, less opaque than human plasma, and more vulnerable. The sun affects all blood. In the daylight, the cells of mine begin to break down, shatter. The radiation of the sun, which would kill you if you were close enough to it, can kill me from a distance.

I moved around behind the blue and violet blinds all afternoon, all around the house, downstairs, upper floor, the attics, looking out through the blue and violet glare, checking to see that he had gone, that he hadn't come back.

He went toward Hammerlake, walking. Even through the blinds, he was definite, indissoluble. He must have known I'd be watching. He didn't glance over his shoulder.

Jace Vincent couldn't have known what was in the packet, not till he opened it. Someone had come on the casket in Cassi's bedroom, closed and locked it and mailed it to me, perhaps an unfriendly, painfully honest, self-effacing servant, hence the lack of a covering letter. Or Jace had taken the letter out and destroyed it, or lost it. . . . How had Jace found me? *It's so simple to find anyone you really want to.* I pictured Jace at Cassi's house, or with the Hog; with the patrolmen from the roadblock. Perhaps it was less complex than that. Perhaps Sand had kept in touch with his big brother (real brother) and there was a communication which mentioned me and Hammerhead. And what does everyone get? Mail. Jace and the mailman, a league of gentlemen against that dreaded witch, a woman alone. A woman who opened the door in her wrapper, who had visitors in cars with Ares digit panels.

And did any of that matter?

What mattered was that Jace Vincent had followed Sand to me. Probably from off-planet, for he had a glaze on him of recent other places, other globes. (Gall Vulcan, where he had nursed and sweated Sand out of the mescadrine D.T.'s?) Again, extraneous. He was here.

What now?

He couldn't be sure. He couldn't know Sand was in trouble, let alone dead. But Sand had often been in trouble. How did Jace know that anything at all was seriously wrong? Force of habit?

An itch in his brother-bone?

See you, he said.

And I couldn't call for help. I'd have to help myself. But there was only one way I knew of, and I couldn't return to that. I was being punished for that now.

The angel-gladiator, the winged avenger.

The house spontaneously self-locked, doors, windows. My mother's installation. No one could get in, at least not without a fight.

Perhaps he'd just wanted to rattle me. I thought I'd convinced him I was impervious; perhaps, therefore, guiltless. He'd just been testing me. He might not come back.

See you.

What had he said to the police, if he'd spoken to them? What had he said to the Hog, or Cassi's servants, or the mailman?

Was there some signal he and Sand had had between them, something missing, by which he knew Sand was dead?

The day crawled by. The sun flared and went out and the night closed its blind over the sky. I closed Cassi's casket in an empty drawer of my vanity table. Out of sight, out of mind? I sat in the parlor, so tense the muscles ached at the base of my skull, between my shoulder blades. I sat there and listened and waited. I couldn't go out. *He* was out there, somewhere.

I could move away from Hammerhead. There were other wildernesses.

It's so simple to find anyone you really want to. (Wherever they may be.)

See you.

When the morning sun came back, Jace Vincent hadn't. He was making me wait, a master musician, for the crash of chords, the brazen blare of trumpets.

I showered and changed into a frock. I put on stockings and shoes, which I hardly wore around the house or on the Plateau.

The door had a lectro-alarm, one of those force bars you can trigger to keep anyone from crossing through the open door, save the occupants. It hadn't been activated since my mother's time, but now I jammed a battery in the slot and switched it on.

As I was standing by the door, I heard the growl of a vehicle taking the spin-off track from the road and gunning for the house.

The center of my body, everything that held me straight, seemed to gush away, but I was still standing.

I'd have to open the door. To leave the door shut would be an admission of fear, and if you were afraid, you went to the police. I couldn't, and therefore I couldn't reveal that I had any reason to. I had to play it that he was just a crazy event in my life that I'd cope with.

The vehicle pulled up, and then there was a pause, then feet, over the ground, up the steps. Feet heavy on the porch. A shadow blossomed on the door glass.

It wasn't his shadow. I could tell immediately. In a way, I'd known they weren't his footfalls.

The buzzer went. I walked stiffly to the door and opened it. A boy about fifteen, in white overalls, was on the porch. He carried a crystal box, a transparent coffin full of green Savior roses.

"Miss Kerwow?"

"That's not my name."

"It isn't?" Concerned, the boy gazed at the docket on the box. His eyes had a puffy, almost tearful look of disorientation. He was at the age of confusion, when you can only get by through a series of perviously planned moves dependent on predicted responses. A reaction out of sequence could derail. I'd been meant to cry out Why, yes, and make a balcony of my arms and breast for the flowers. Then he could have smiled (what a charming boy!) and we would both have been satisfied. But now he fumbled at the docket, two wheels off the track. "It says, it says Kerwow here."

"Is there a sender's name?" He didn't guess his panic was one-ninetieth of mine.

"Sure is. J. Vincent."

"Take them away."

"But Miss Kerwow—"

"My name is not Kerwow."

"Lady, they're special delivery. They cost twenty-three credits, plus delivery charge—"

His eyes were bulging. He would never go. He would stand there forever, until the green blooms wilted into brown, and the natural-cloth overalls turned to skeletal rags on his body.

I made a balcony.

"All right. Give them to me—"

Something snapped. He didn't need pre-planning for a second, indignation was enough.

"Well don't do me any favors, lady."

I didn't tip him. I shut the door. He was fifteen and working on Mature Studies and he needed cash. But Jace had sent the flowers.

I put the transparent coffin on the floor. I had the same feeling I had with Cassi's casket.

But nothing exploded, there wasn't a message. Somehow, I didn't need a message. You lay flowers on a grave.

They were beautiful, the roses. That was my problem, I wanted to destroy them because they came from him, they're poison. But they were not poison, they were loveliness. So I siphoned out water and set them in one of my mother's pottery bowls. I'd thank him graciously when he came.

I waited in the kitchen then. Through the blind of the kitchen window I could see the broken swing, the orange tree where the man beat and raped me and escaped alive. What was his name?

The flower vehicle had driven away, and now it seemed to come back and the buzzer went.

My hands were shaking, heart booming.

But still it was not his shadow on the door.

"Miss Kervac, I have a crate of wine for you."

J. Vincent had sent me a crate of wine. It cost him two hundred credits. I wouldn't let them in. I made them leave it on the porch. Before they drove off, I brought out the green roses in the pottery bowl and placed them by the crate. I didn't deny that I was called Kervak. There was no message.

I sat on the wooden floor in the hall, to one side, out of the window splotch. I wasn't thinking. My heart thudded slow and heavy. You drink wine at funerals.

The door buzzed.

"Miss Kweet?"

I broke. I laughed. It's funny, it's hilarious. And he'd sent me a three-foot white-velvet bear. You unpop the bear's guts and a white flagon of scent emerges on a satin ledge. The bear's eyes are cold; cold blue eyes. Like a snake's.

I closed the door and doubled over and retched. But I was dried up inside, a burned-out ditch.

Presumably he wasn't sure of me. I might be on the level, an honest nobody. I might yet call the police in Hammerlake. So he threatened me with gifts I can't complain of. Fragrance to perfume the dead. Frankincense and myrrh.

Then I waited again. I waited all afternoon. Sometimes the house creaks and my pulses stumble. I could call the Hog: You're the lawyer, uncle. Well, there's a man pestering me. The Hog wouldn't want to know, or he'd want to know too much.

When he comes back, you'll have to, Sabella. Have to kill him. Which means you act friendly, you watch the lodestone have its effect on him, as on all the others. All you have to do is briefly want him. Is it so hard? His skin is flawless golden wood and his hair is jet. His blood's blood-color. Air to breathe, Sabella, *air*.

But there's something—something. He frightens me too much. I don't want to touch him, go near him. He frightens me.

Think of the man under the orange tree. You could have taken him any time. You held off, not because you were afraid, though you were terrified, but because you didn't want the guilt of his life. Remember?

You can kill this one. It's guiltless. It's self-defense.

When he comes back.

Out on the porch in the westering light, the wine bottles glinted, the roses withered, the white bear stared.

There was a wind blowing up, like the day I returned from Ares, the day before the night Sand found me.

Dust to dust, ashes to ashes, Sand to—sand.

But Jace wasn't dust, isn't sand, isn't jet and wood and metal. He was skin and muscle, bone, fiber, juices, enzymes, atoms. Nobody made him up. He wasn't like all the rest. He was real.

I won't answer the door again.

I left the bar switched on and I went up the stairs and lay down under the gauze curtains of my bed.

Paternoster. . . .

Sleeping—suddenly the room was black. It was night, inside and out. There was a noise. Someone was knocking on the glass door below.

Glass doesn't break any more, unless it's custom-built to do so. He'd know that. Why knock when the buzzer was there?

I lay quiet and waited for the knocking to cease. It

didn't, it went on and on. O.K., I can take the sound. Rap your bloody knuckles raw, you bastard.

Then, a girl's voice was shrieking.

I sat up, swung my legs off the bed. Certain reactions have to be learned, like those of the fifteen-year-old boy. A girl shrieking on my porch may mean different trouble, worse trouble. Once, in Hammerlake, a police patrol questioned me on the street because two girls had been fighting in the bar I had walked out of. This one shrieks again, and now I can make out the single word: "Hey! Hey! Hey!"

My night vision was developed long ago, and starlight comes in to help me through the stained window above the stairs, showing me the door, and a white shadow this time, thrown close on the glass. She can't see me, the shrieking girl. She knocks again, rat-tat.

He had sent her, this girl. She was out there with the wine and the flowers and the perfume-belly bear.

The fear was mounting up in me, the great orchestra.

The knocking, on and on and on, point counterpoint.

"Hey! Hey!"

I ran down the stairs; I didn't mean to. As I ran, I hit my fist against the old-fashioned light switch, a nipple in a lily bud, on the wall. Light burst through the hall, against the glass door, and my pupils squeezed to dots, but I still saw her. It was me. Sabella, when she was sixteen, seventeen, eighteen, low-cut dress, white powdered flesh, bleached hair, red nails. A vamp, (I perceived the ironic pun) a harlot from Hammerlake. How would he know what I looked like at seventeen?

I buttoned the door, and it swung wide, and I was face to face, eye to eye with Me. I don't mean she was my double. She was my past, is all. My past, that never ended.

"Hey," she said again, between perplexity and outrage, "Is this a *party?*"

Then she took in my face. Do I look like that? She

backed a step and demanded loudly of the darkness; "Jay-yaice."

They must have walked from the road, for there was no car on the track, shutting out the stairs. But as he moved from the lacework bench, he shut them out. He had on black again, but different clothes, no sunglasses, just the black glass eyes themselves.

"Why," he said, "if it isn't my friend Jezebel."

I'm standing in the doorway. The lectro-chain's switched on and he can see the faint glow of it, and that this is as far as he gets.

"Is she welcoming?" Jace Vincent inquired.

"I should say not," said the bleached girl.

"What about my advance payment?" said Jace. "Why, I anticipated finding you, Jezebella, sipping my wine, carrying my roses, smelling like sixty credits a bottle. And look," he showed me a wad of credits in his hand, the bills you rarely see in a world of check and auto-cards. "Down payment. More to come. For services to be rendered. Or have the charges gone up since my brother was here?"

I didn't say anything.

The girl sensed abruptly that this candy had a bitter kernel.

"Jay-yaice? You said there'd be a pa-arty."

"Shut up," he told her companionably. "Unless you want to remind this lady of the going rate of whores."

"Jay-yaice—"

"You scared she'll call someone? A patrol, maybe. She won't. Not my old friend Jezebella. My kid brother told me about this one. She's hot stuff. She does it like nobody else."

With strange profundity, his harlot told him, "Nobody does it like nobody else."

Jace directed his hand, mildly, as if to reach in at me, and the lectro-chain sizzled up, prepared to block him. He smiled at me, as before, politely. Then he leaned and hefted the wine crate, agile, as if it weighed a quarter of what it did. He nodded to the girl. "The rest of it's yours."

"Oh," said the girl, and her face was a child's face. "Can I have the bear, too?"

"Sure," he said.

She struggled and succeeded and had the bear and the roses, and she looked happy and very young. She'd forgotten me.

They walked away into the night as if nothing had happened, and he whistled a hymn tune, giving a lick to it it never had in church.

The car—Jace's?—revved about two-thirds down the track.

Green petals rushed along the porch.

The sun came up in a great mulberry ball and golden razors lanced the blinds. I lay on my bed and listened to the sun raining on the house, the tindery crackle it made, hitting the joists, the paint, the emanations. I felt enormously calm because there was no point in anything else. I had something in the freezer that would keep me going two or three days more. I had hash grains and tobacco and fruit juice and air-conditioning and music. I didn't need to go out. I didn't need to open the door. I could lie there, taking my time, making up my mind. And when I was ready, I could invite him in. I'd be glad to, then.

When something cracked on my window, I thought of Easterly. Boys used to do that in easterly, to wake you, little crumble stones flung at the glass.

"Oh, Miss Kwhore."

His voice was more familiar than my mother's, which had faded in my memory.

"Oh, Miss Kwhore, you have a very stylish residence."

Something smashed. Breakable glass—a bottle left over from the wine crate? If he'd been close all night, I never heard him.

"Yes, Miss Kweer, I'd say you had a fine appreciating property."

I half sat, then dropped back. I was going to look out at him. Silly.

The second time he spoke, he'd moved slightly, and then again, but I couldn't hear his steps. He walked soft, the way I can walk, a hunter's way.

And then he struck something with a stone, sounding it. It was away around the other side of the house, the tree side. I couldn't think what he struck, but suddenly he was at my side again, under my window.

"You have some charming antiquated features here."

And I knew what he'd struck, and slowly I sat up again, and I held my breath.

"Shit, Miss Kwack, you even have an incinerator."

And now I understood what it's like to be changed to stone. The limbs too heavy to move, the rib cage jammed so no oxygen will come, the eyes starting, the tongue grown into the roof of the mouth.

The silence outside told nothing. A stone can't ask, can't go to a window and see.

And then I heard his footsteps, he'd turned up the volume for my benefit. A deft crunching over the ground, and with it a low thin electronic humming, some machine that was trundling beside him up from the track. He walked with the machine, around to the back.

Suddenly the hum broke into a great chugging noise, a whoosh, and a vibration that ran through the frame of the house. And he too broke suddenly into a huge hoarse singing shout:

> "Oh when we get there,
> When we get there to that glor-yus town, o'gold
> Jezus'll be waiting,
> Oh yes Jezus'll be waiting—"

I picked up my stone body and moved.

Momma's bedroom looks out toward the orange tree. I can remember her pale face watching me as I swung the swing. I hadn't gone in her room for five years. I buttoned the door, and it was like cutting into a loaf of time, through a crust, through bread. And even though the dust-eaters and the air-conditioning did their work here as in the rest of the house, the atmosphere was thick as bread. I didn't look at anything. Only out the window, the one window that had no blind, merely the yellow gauze in front of it. The sunlight was like a knife, and the noise of the machine was roaring through the floor.

"Oh yeah, Jezus'll be waitin' as the Holy Book foretold."

A black rubber pipe went in the earth ten feet from the kitchen door. It quivered. It was attached to a cube of machinery with a blow-out chimney on the top, and an open rear end. I couldn't see Jace. I could see a haze of gray and black cinders showering out fine as pollen from the rear end of the machine. The machine was pumping out the belly of the pit under the incinerator.

. . . conturbata sunt omnia ossa mea . . .

I was running out of the room. No, not this way.

Brush your hair, Sabella. Straighten your dress. Put on your shoes. You look sick, Sabella, but for thirteen years I never saw you look less than beautiful. Pick up the half cigarette in the tray, light it. That's it. *Now*, run.

I switched off the lectro-chain and went out into the molten clamor of the morning and around the house. As if I had all the hours there are.

This side of the machine, Jace was. He stripped to black jeans, his body like a living carving, the round brazen muscles gliding in his arms as he manually shoveled through the piles of settled cinders. He'd left off singing. His face was concentrated, but though I'd made no sound, he knew I'd come out, and he turned and straightened up, and then he grinned.

"Hallo, Miss Kerwale."

"Hallo, Jace."

His face didn't alter, but he said, politely correcting me, "My name is Jason, Miss Kerwule. Only my friends call me Jace."

"And my name is Sabella, Jason."

Pleasantly he said, "Your name's just shit to me."

"Jason," I said. I looked in his eyes. They were hard, like the sun. "What are you doing?"

"Just sorting your dry compost, Miss Kerville. You see, a lady on her own can eat only so much, particularly a skinny jane like you. But a lady and a man. Some things don't burn. Metal tops, the check stamp on cartons, meat bones. I'd say you'd had a guest, Miss Kweele. Like my buddy the mailman told me."

I seemed to be looking at him down a funnel. He appeared small and made by an able craftsman. My nausea was a kind of feathering through my whole body. But he couldn't see it.

"I sometimes have guests, Jason."

"I thought you did, Miss Kwole."

The machine gave a sort of hiccup. Something a little too big for the pipe was being lugged up, sucked in. The dust would whirl off the top of the pit first, then the lighter noncumbustibles, the metal bits he spoke of. Down below, where the soil-returning mulch had begun, the machine wouldn't take hold. Between the two lay the heavier unburnt leftovers of the furnace. The pipe bucked a fraction, coughed, renewed its grip. Like a dog worrying a bone—

"Jason, leave that. Come in the house."

"Suddenly the lady is gregarious."

"Last night . . . just wasn't the right time, Jason."

Go to him, Sabella. Go closer.

I could scent him, and he was like Sand, a clean masculine odor, unmistakable, potent. In fact, he was very like Sand, but Sand crystallized, fused into essentials and into strength. Sand's weakness drew me to him. All their weaknesses. But this one wasn't weak.

The pipe gurgled.

He glanced at it. I was close enough to reach out and run my finger across his skin. Chest and belly were like sculptured rock. He turned back to me and I lifted my finger away from him.

"What did Sand tell you about me?" I said.

"A couple of things."

"Tell me."

I couldn't see any whites to his eyes, they were so dark and so still.

"Sand has a knack for permanent trouble. We keep in touch because that way I'm ready to bail him out. One stellagram a month, and if anything comes up, an extra stellagram. And he always tells me about the women he runs with. Women are mostly bad luck for Sand. So I know all about you, about Cassilda and Trim and how you turn Sand on and how he's following you to this old colonial house on the Plateau. And how there's two months' nothing from him after that. Which is what you're waiting to find out, Miss Kwek. Why I'm here."

"Do you know all about me, Jason? Why don't you come and see for yourself."

"First, you tell me where Sand is."

He's in that pipe, in that damn pipe, choking it, but it's going to spit him out, any moment, right where you're standing—

"He had something else to do. I don't know what, he didn't tell me. I guess he'll be back. You could wait around."

"He left his car in a tunnel on the Hammerlake Road. There was a girl. You have a sister, Miss Kwade?"

The pipe gave a big choke and dislodged the obstacle.

Black and brown, the sticks of bones hailed down into the dust and cinders.

We were both looking at the bones.

"What the hell is that?" His voice had changed. For a second there was no strength, no assurance in it after all.

"Oh God, how horrible," I said. "My dog. He got sick and he died. I had to burn his body."

The blazing day had turned to paper. Rose aluminum sky, reddish floor of congealed parchment. The man, a paper cutout, with drawn-in shaded musculature, hair and features.

"A dog," he said.

Then the machine vomited out something else. It ripped over the paper sky and landed, and skidded. It skidded to our feet. It was unrecognizable, blackened, jagged. But there was a dull glowing smear on it, like melted debased metal. Jace Vincent bent forward a little. Now he could make out the curious wedge-shaped formation in the middle of the smear, and the two calcified burned drops that glared up out of it.

It was Sand's snake, the gold jewelry around his neck, what was left of it. And the two blue gem eyes of the snake, no longer blue, were still unclosed.

There wasn't any time anymore. There was leisure to let my gaze drift up to Jace's profile. His face had gone yellow. He couldn't have known it all, then. Of course, it was terrible to learn this way. I felt an instinctive, momentary idiotic pity, and then I remembered that I was part of this.

I sprang and I spun and I ran. I'd run after the wolves. I was quick. The open door was only around the side of the house.

I could see the door, I was twenty feet away, when he brought me down, his weight like thunder, like a lion.

The ground hit me, the ground crammed into my mouth and thrust into my breasts, and the man lay on me like stone, and then he pulled off and I was flung around, onto my back.

He knelt over me. His face wasn't vulnerable anymore; how could I ever have reckoned it was? It was the face of God turned toward Gomorrah.

I brought up my hands and scratched at his face and jackknifed my knees into his stomach and his groin—but somehow his flesh eluded me, it wasn't there. He caught my hands and impaled them on the earth and he lay over my legs. I arched and strained my throat, but even my mouth couldn't come near him now. He said into my face, without expression, "So you killed him. How and why?"

When my voice came, I was surprised, it was hoarse and naked with terror. I screamed at him.

"You wouldn't believe me if I told you."

"Listen," he said, "I know that murder has become a sickness, and the Planetary Federation puts murderers in doll houses on a hill with pretty flowers and trees to make them happy. I know that. So this is our business, Jezebel. Yours and mine. Nobody is going to rescue you and institutionalize you and keep you safe. You have to deal with me."

I didn't fight anymore. The sun was washing me away like mud from a lake shore. I was blind, I was quiet, and blindly, quietly I said, "Sand was sick. I tried to take him to the hospital outside Hammerlake, but there was a roadblock and they checked the car and Sand wandered away and he died. I didn't want to get involved."

"Don't pass out," he says. "I'll only bring you around and we'll start again."

I was whispering, with my eyes shut tight.

"*De profundis clamavi ad te, Domine . . .*"

"Stop that," he said. He slapped my face lightly, wanting to keep me with him.

"*Domine, exaudi vocem meam.*"

He held my hair, not really painfully, and repeated to me in English, "*Out of the depths I have cried to you, O Lord: hear my voice*. The only one who's going to hear you is me, Jezebel."

"Please take me in the house."

I didn't really think he would, but he did. He picked me up and carried me. He put me on the floor exactly where my mother lay when she was dead, under the crimson spillage of the window, and I wondered how he knew to do that, or if he knew.

I was listless. Was I afraid? Probably.

He didn't need a special weapon or ritual to kill me. Anything would do. A gun, a cord, a blow.

"What you're doing to yourself, Bel," my mother said, standing over me with her sad and fallen face.

"I know, momma."

I'm crying, momma.

"I know, momma."

I'm crying.

2

When I found the pendant, it was a few days after my eleventh birthday, and it was the day I started to bleed. My father had been dead for nine years, and our house was a woman's world. Women tend, as do men, to turn into clans when thrown in with too many of their own gender, and then those clans practice mysteries. From my tenth birthday on there'd have been these mystery hintings: *Once you start. Once you get to be a big girl, Bel.* I knew about menstruation, school took care of that. But somehow the science had never fully related to my body. A picture on a screen was just a picture on a screen. Then one day the picture happened inside me. Even when you know, it shocks. Even when you understand it's nothing bad, somehow it's still bad. Now you're different, not yourself anymore. In that moment, I turned for reassurance, applause perhaps, I turned to find myself in the eyes of another, because this is where generally human beings find themselves. But my mother gave me a tape book to play which told me what I had to do now, although I'd already heard it through at school. So I went out of town and along the road over the hidden mines and by the refineries and over the river into the meadows. Where a couple of the old dry canals opened under the rosy sands of Easterly's neck of the deserts, that still make up four-fifths of Novo Mars, I found a hole in the ground.

Anice (or is it Alicia?) fell into a hare's warren. Do bats eat cats she wondered, as she plunged into the dark. I suppose Sabella had climbed trees, dug into holes; I don't recall. I think I'd even seen this hole before, assumed it was but another pit in the quarry that overhung the canal bed. Why did I go in? I foresee an analogy, the womb of the earth, Sabella's womb. But I think it was just somewhere to hide, and maybe Alicia's was also a hiding place from her womanhood. Certainly, the tunnel had no exclusive feminine aura. In fact, an old catapult, the sometime gadget of most Easterly boys, lay near the entrance, but when I knelt on it it broke, brittle with age.

When I dreamed about the tunnel on the plane to Ares, my mother was there, but when it happened she hadn't been, I was alone. Nor were there tall thin pillars, as at Dawson, or up in the Calicoes. The tunnel roof was actually low, and I didn't go far before I came on a slab of rock set endways across the tunnel. All this I discerned by feel, because my body had shut out most of the light that came in at the entrance. Even then, I thought the slab was a grave.

The rock of the slab was worn or planed as smooth as satin, and, as with the other ruins of New Mars, there was no sand blown in, no dust, except their own, as if they had had dust-eaters at work. I was stroking the texture of the smooth rock when my fingers found a crevice. In the crevice was a pebble, also silken smooth.

When I took it out and held it toward the light, trying to see, it was opaque and dull, the shape and size of a small plum. But at the narrow end was a ring fixed through the stone. I was only eleven but I recognized the metal of that ring, the amalgam they christened areum, stuff of meteors that die here, unreproducible.

So I bore my prize out into the sunlight, holding it in my closed fist.

By planetary law, an item discovered on the site of a previous civilization is Federation property, which means property of Earth. I knew that, but I wasn't about to renounce what the day had given me when it had already taken away so much.

I sat in the rough meadows beyond the dam, and

picked the stone up, and held it, and put it down. It was ugly, but pleasing to touch and caress.

I watched the sun dive off the slope of the world, and then I got up to hurry home. I had my first cramps, and the tape book had recommended which analgesics were the best. When I was into town, I stopped at the drug store. I had been sentenced but I knew my rights.

On the street, as I started to smell the aniseed grass of our lawn, I looked at the stone, and it wasn't dull any more. It was clear and bright as crystal, as diamond, its facets all inside and winking, blinking back at the stars.

I made a deduction. The heat of my hands and my palm's pressure had burnished the stone free of sediment.

My mother hadn't told me I was wonderful to become a woman, so I didn't tell her about the stone.

I saved my expense money, and I bought a chain of white metal at a store on the far side of town. I never wore the stone then, except in my bedroom. Then I let it rest against my skin, between my breasts, which were growing fast now. I felt secretive when I wore the stone, and sensual and afraid and—as if I hungered, but I didn't know for what until that night when I was fourteen.

Six months before I was fourteen, I'd started to wear the stone all the time. Other girls wore crosses or medallions or good-luck pieces. The stone was mine. Nobody saw it. When I had to go into the school shower or the changing room, I'd have an adhesive tape wrapped round the stone. The girls laughed at that. They didn't like me. I was different, I didn't have a father, and their mothers didn't like mine because she was a widow with a bit of ephemeral money and maybe she'd seduce their men, so the daughters, catching the virus unconsciously, didn't care for me either. And now that I was beautiful they liked me less and less. And strangely, the boys didn't like me any more than the girls did. I didn't look soft or alluring or yielding or admiring at them. I was too beautiful to be pretty.

I didn't really know why I was on the highway near the beer shop that night. Restlessness, hunger. When the boy picked me up, I was flattered and amazed. He had very blue eyes and fair hair and he self-drove a car. He said we'd go to a cinemat, and to a roadhouse and dance. But he parked by the road under great dripping fern trees.

I knew about sex, too. We all did. We were taught about it and then told to leave it alone. The boy explained with his hands and his mouth that it wasn't to be left alone. I was excited, and then I felt the stone, pulsing against my breast. I became so fascinated by the pulsing of the stone, I lost track of what the boy did to me, all the burning sensations passing into each other, the stone their focus. And then he laid me on my back and he tried me, and when he couldn't ride easy, he forced me instead. It wasn't that I attempted to prevent him, but I felt roughly torn like a garment and the scald of blood. He'd taught me to kiss, the kiss that draws the blood against the skin. His neck was against my mouth. It was natural. I took his flesh into my mouth, and my teeth met through the vein. When he screamed out, I thought it was in pain. He was holding my arm, and he bruised it black; the other hand was clutched on the seat beneath us, and his nails went in the fabric. He was crying oh God, oh God, oh God, and then he didn't cry any more, and only the movements of his body went on, and then even they stopped.

I was satiated and drowsy and I lay there half an hour under him before I comprehended he was dead. I had continued too long, you see. I hadn't known.

I stopped menstruating when I was fourteen, about the time my body recognized I was no longer human.

"Is there some reason why you haven't killed me?" I said to Jace Vincent.

"There's a good reason why I might."

I couldn't see him. My eyes were still dazzled from the sun, though the dark glasses helped. He had let me put them on; at least he didn't stop me. There were no tears in my stockings, because nylon doesn't run any more, but there were runs in the long pale calves of my legs, and across my hands. I needed to replace what the sun had done to me out there. But it hardly mattered, if he was going to kill me. The fact was, he didn't want to kill me, not yet. He wanted to get the truth, or he thought he did. He wanted his vengeance drawn out, to break my back and watch me squirm, because he imagined I was a whore-lady who killed his brother for cash or kicks, and in a way he was right.

Presently I said, "Can I have some water?"

He didn't speak.

I didn't add anything, and then he got up and got my wrist and pulled me with him into the kitchen. I fell against the siphon unit. My fingers were cotton wool and I couldn't make the button work, so then he did it for me.

"What's the matter with you?"

"What does it look like?"

"It looks like let's pretend."

I drank the water, which nearly came back, but didn't. "Maybe I'm just afraid of you."

"It's more than that."

"I have photophobia. I can't take much sun."

"I know about photophobia. You don't have the right symptoms."

That's funny. I laugh, and he shakes me and lifts and holds me against the wall.

"Now, you tell me what you did to Sand, Photophobella."

My eyes are getting clear. I can focus on his golden throat. It would be easy. *Do* it.

I can't.

Why can't I?

"I told you, Sand was sick. I tried—"

"To take him to a hospital. Yeah. What did he have? Something he caught off you?"

I could see the orange tree through the blind.

"Let me down. I'll tell you everything."

I didn't know what I was doing, half-blind, dizzy. My instinct was, of course, still to run, but by day my escape route had to be limited. When he swung me down and let go of me, my instinct nevertheless mastered me stupidly.

I wasn't unexpected or fast anymore, I simply pushed by him and floundered out of the kitchen, toward the stairs, and up through the daggers of stained glass sun. He let me do this, although I had told him nothing, and I was aware that he let me. When I fell and pulled myself on hands and knees, he let me do that too. I had only one direction to go. I went into the bedroom, and thrust the door shut, and buttoned the lock. All that he allowed, but only in order to prove it was futile.

As I lay on the bed, stunned and mindless and panting with the effort, I heard that soft step of his that he permitted me to hear when he wanted me to. Then he put his shoulder to my door, a dazzling brazen machine, and the lock sizzled and shorted and the door crashed inward.

"Just so you know," he said.

I'm so tired. Suppose I told him the real truth. I killed your brother for his blood. He was beautiful. I couldn't get enough of him, I drank him nearly dry and his heart stopped because he loved what I did to him too much.

"I don't think we can go any further with this," I said.

"You don't."

"Because I told you the truth and you won't accept what I've told you."

"I can accept that Sand was working for the old guy, Trim, and that maybe Sand dug up some news you didn't want printed. Cyanide between bread and butter might be something you're good at."

"Would I tell you if I were?"

"You might," he said. "You see, Jezebel, you're

curling at the edges. I don't know what you're on, but there's some kind of stuff you have to have, and until you get it, you're shaking. When you start to shake enough, you'll tell me anything I want."

I could feel my mouth idiotically form into a grin.

Yes, I believe I am exhibiting the symptoms of drug addiction and deprivation, sufficient anyway to convince him, whose brother screamed and rolled on the floor from a lack of mescadrine.

"So I'll finally tell you I murdered Sand, and *then* you'll kill me."

"Don't worry," he said. "You have religion. I'll let you pray first."

"That's very kind." But he had already turned. "Suppose," I said, "suppose I have a secret stash of whatever drug it is you think I'm using, up here in this room?"

He turned back, and in his helpful voice he said, "If you do, then you'll use it, and that way I'll know. Then I'll rip the room apart and I'll find it. And then we'll wait till you start to need again." He went out, and from the place beyond the broken swinging door he said, "On the other hand, I reckon you have it ready-mixed in your freezer, like any store-minded junkie."

Don't flinch, don't move. Don't say a word.

Five minutes later, I hear cans explosing in the kitchen below, and the glub-glub of the waste-pipe, drinking the fruit juice he's pouring away. When the glass container falls, I hear that too. Unlike the glass of doors or windows or goblets, the container is disposable and smashes, and the red *eau de vie* will be gliding on the kitchen floor, amid the fragments of the glass. Presently the sun will dry the substance into a rich raw stain, just like blood.

"Say good-bye," he called up to me.

I said good-bye.

I need, I need. Every part of me is a hurt, my joints, my stomach, my tongue, my glands, my eyes. The sun took and I can't replace the sun's taking. I'm dying. No, not yet.

I lay on the bed. The sun was out. (Where did the day go to?) Sometime earlier he went down by the road where his car was parked, and brought back a pack of ready-food, which he heated in momma's old microwave-heater . Then he brought me a dish of this amalgam and urged me cheerfully to eat it. He only removed the plate when I informed him what would happen if he didn't. He offered me wine, too. Wine, he pointed out solicitously, would blunt the edge of the knife in my guts, for a while. His sadism was affectionate and intense, and under it he was a blank, not enjoying it at all, just using it, like the rack, the jump-chair, to get my confession.

Two hours after sunset, the first wolf let out his whistling howl, high on the razor-back hills in the star storm of night.

When I heard the howl my whole body began to jerk and tremble. I started to groan aloud and couldn't hold the sounds inside myself as agony and craving flung me about the bed. Then all the wolves in the world were howling out there, as if they called to me: Come, come, come to us, why do you wait?

Soon he reappeared in my door, dark on darkness, one glowing star caught between his lips.

"Charming cigarettes you have," he said. White smoke curled from his mouth as he spoke, and I smelled the incense smell of the loaded tobacco. He crossed to the window, passed by the mirror, raised the blind, and buttoned up the glass. The tide of wolf voices sang into the room, making it tingle, sparkle, like winter frost forming on everything.

Jace watched me.

"You like that sound?"

"Yes."

He moved around the bed and offered me the cigarette.

"No." I turned my head aside.

"You're hurting, honey," he said. "Very bad. Aren't you?"

"You know I am."

"Say a little prayer," he said, and he went away again.

Why can't I get over this unseen barrier and take him and have him?

The voices of the wolves were fading, blowing away. Out there, the hills are promises, there are four thousand neons in heaven.

Maybe he'd sleep. Sometime he had to. He was confident, he thought he'd beaten me.

The house was softly dislocating its tensions in the chill of the young night. Momma's ghost was sitting in her room, watching at the window. The broken swing and the broken door slowly swung to and fro in the wind.

The knife moved like a child in my belly, but then I began to drift, drift up out of the hurt. I began gently to hallucinate, or to dream. . . .

About how, over westward, Montiba way, the little deer may be feeding on the night-black plants, and how sometimes the heavy cattle, white as plaster in the dark, break their way from the corrals. . . .

Where do the wolves run to who hunt these hills, where do they run when they're invisible—back into time, before the civilization of this planet ended? Back to when the pillars upheld roofs like fluted water-ice and the urns were empty?

Dreaming, I struck west and ran ten miles. It was nearly midnight by the rings and spirals of the stars which seem immovable yet move. (No. The planet moves, not the stars. We must ignore the evidence of our eyes.)

There was a ravine, a memory ravine I remembered at once, its contours, its tiers ripe with leaves. A fragmentary wind rustled the papers of the leaves, and below, a rivulet of black water waded. I eased down through the shadows, and I could feel the dream deer as I always felt them, like a warmth in the night.

Near the bottom of the ravine side, where the eucalyptus trees grew sideways toward the water, I beheld the deer by the river, like young girls in a story, like Pharaoh's daughter at the river with her handmaids. No male in attendance, for the season is far off. Now a slender head, ears like curled leaves, lifts and listens. How lovely, the striped body, the fragile legs. Every one of them's a porcelain figurine.

I walked forward, and other heads lifted. The stone was burning softly on my breast, and I loved the deer as I moved among them. When I was fourteen, fifteen, and learned my hunting, I was surprised that I could go right into the herd like this, selecting from them the one I would drink from, like a precious wine stored in a vase of flesh. When I took from the deer, there was no human sexual act to encounter, to use as bait and placation. There was simply their instinct to fly from me, which only the chosen animal would exhibit. If they died, it was from shock, blood loss. I killed accidentally, through greed and carelessness, at first. And then I lessoned myself in how I need not kill. On the night of Cassi's death, I had chosen mistakenly a creature which had a weakness in it, and when it died between my hands, it was as though Cassi's cold breath, hissing from her corpse, had condemned us all. The deer, Sand, myself.

Here is the one I will have.

She comes after me instantly, her delicate steps pattering on the stones among the moss by the water. She came trustingly at first, irresistibly. In reality, I would feel now the excitement of hunger, and tenderness, compassion. In the dream, my limbs are leaden. I creep to the edge of the clearing, and in the cradle of the eucalyptus I drop down, and the deer follows me.

A yard away her struggle begins. She suddenly knows. She's come to the wolf. She tosses her head and stamps her miniature feet, as if she were tethered to a post, scenting death, unable to escape.

I go on gazing at her, at her soft antimony eyes, and finally she comes on again and kneels down. Her head lowers itself. Her eyes are glazed with terror, but her body is quiescent. Don't be afraid. I stroke her neck, whose nap is prickly velvet, (I can feel it, even dreaming.) Her smell is strong but healthy, (I can smell her, dreaming). My eyeteeth are slanted a fraction, outward, not enough to notice, enough to save my own mouth from their razors, (dreaming, I can analyze.) I make the single bite with enormous care. I must be very careful of her life. When I begin to draw out the wine, she quivers, tenses. Now she's ready for flight the moment I negate the hypnosis I've set on her. She feels, I think, nothing. She suffers it because she must. While I feel gratitude, comfort and boundless love.

Measure, Sabella. Don't drain her. Don't harm her. Love her and thank her. Let her go. (I don't remember any more that it's a dream).

No more, Sabella.

Let her go.

I wrench my head away, and at once the deer leaps to her feet. Memory of a hundred other deer.

They flash like bolts from a gun, through the nets of the shadows and the leaves, over the stream. The strong deer, who, when they had put distance between us, would rest and browse again, their cells refashioning what I had robbed them of. All the deer vaulted over the water and poured through unseen holes in the black.

The moss made a pillow for my body, and the pains were going out in me as if cancelled by a powerful analgesic, that yet left my brain quite lucid. I have evaded the avenger. How had I done that?

Perhaps, I had not.

I lay there in the dream and I thought, *he couldn't keep up with me, a wolf-bitch's running.*

But he was an athlete, his body gave evidence of that. He could keep up. Silently. But a night is full of sounds, of winds and grass and sands and waters. What you take for silence in the hills is only another kind of clamor. Yes. Jace could have tracked me, could have witnessed me. If I sat up and I saw him in the nightscape anywhere around me, then I'd know I'd told him every detail, after all.

There were none of the breaks, the edited sequences that come in dreams. All went forward logically, in progression. So I sat. And just across the trickle of the stream, the way the deer had fled, a black silhouette was inked on the night. It was not a freak form constructed of boulder, tree or shadow. It was a man. It was Jace.

I sat and looked at him, and eventually I could even see his eyes, their brightness, and then I could see the sheen of something slung behind his shoulder, a burnished tube that also was no part of any tree or branch; the long muzzle of an electric gun with which a man goes hunting wolves.

Dream Jace spoke to me.

"And that," he said, "the thing with the deer, is what you did to Sand."

"That and more." I wasn't afraid, not here, not in the dream-canyon, pain-freed, among the stars and the leaves.

I got to my feet. I was warm, and still, and easy with him.

"When I take blood from a man," I said softly, "it isn't the same as when I take it from an animal. When I find a man I want, when we make love; I take it then."

I was walking to him, I was stepping over the narrow stream. My tongue gently burning. My body burning. All the night was strung, like the strings of violins, resin-taut. As I walked to Jace, stepping over the water, I was like a bow, ten bows or twenty, drawn across those strings. And the note sounded deep in the womb of the darkness.

"Let me show you," I said to him. I knelt down before the man with the gun as the deer knelt to me. I was arching my back and the hoarse music of the night was soaring through me. He could kill me then. I didn't care. I wanted him to.

I turned my head, and offered him my neck.

"It's all right," Sand said. "You're awake. It's all right now."

But it wasn't Sand. There was nobody there. No one by me.

The wind was blowing the curtains around my bed, the wind which smelled of the hills and which had brought me my dream. But not all of my dream.

About me, the house was quiet as though empty.

His skin is sunburned, Sabella. He drinks alcohol and eats real food, Sabella, you saw him. No, that isn't the horrible joke. He isn't one of your own kind. You're still unique, and alone.

Why then. . . .

I was the victim. *Willing* victim.

It's sex, Sabella. What you missed. What you give but never receive. That's why you're afraid to touch him, Sabella.

I rested my head against my knees, doubled up to ease the clawing in my stomach. And I smiled coldly, remembering the Freudian dream symbol of the gun, and the Pascian symbols of the stream, the violins.

The house was so noiseless. Was he sleeping? Was he? The avenger, doubly my enemy, doubly to be dreaded.

I should like to see him asleep, just once. That face smoothed out, helpless and blind in sleep.

No, Sabella, let me explain this to you. All sadists are also masochists, one indulgence feeds the other. Sand kneeled to you. Now you kneel to the sword. But it's the night you need. Yes, I can, I must.

I crept out, and down those stairs which I've descended a thousand, thousand times. In the starlight from the window, pausing, reaching out to sense and avoid him. The darkness was deaf and dumb with waiting for me, the whole night a pool that I must cleave.

The glass door would open silently at my finger on its button. The night would open silently, and close over my head, hiding me.

The splotch of the starlight window was colorless yet

glowing on the wooden floor. I half turned, intuitively, feeling for the parlor, the sofa where I had slept, and where the man, secure in his assumptions, was sleeping now.

I ran forward soundlessly, and a huge blackness materialized from nothing, apparently from the bottom of the door, and reached out and seized me with iron hands.

I screamed in an ecstasy of terror, my whole body and my spirit dissolved in fear and loathing and despair. Pressed into the shadow, he had waited for me, like a great dog guarding a prison gate. Screaming, I couldn't stop. The whole night was screaming. The wolves, who waited on the hills for me, cheated as I am cheated, reciprocal of my terror, howled.

They were closer than I'd ever heard them, a ring of voices spiking the air, the stars.

"Shut up," he said to me.

I could only scream.

"All right," he said. He was forcing me, upright and wrapped against him, into the kitchen. Lights fired up. He was forcing me to look at something. I couldn't see. Then I opened my eyes.

My mother used to make homemade lemonade in that cut-glass jug. On the lawn at Easterly, lemons and sugar, and I was eleven years old, and I was almost happy and I don't remember—

There was blood in it now, blood flavored with hashish and pomegranates and tomatoes.

"Is that it?" he said to me. "Is that what you want?"

I was breathing and that was enough. He dropped me in a chair and poured a glass of the red juice for me with the detached accuracy of a bartender. It was deduction, he couldn't know. There was more of it than anything else and it had concentrator granules on the container rim. Maybe he understood, too, its scent is a cover for something else. He'd poured it in the jug, then smashed the container so I'd hear.

I drank carefully, almost primly.

My stomach griped, dulled, subsided.

It was over.

The avenger had saved me.

I could feel the imprint of his body against mine, even though he was no longer touching me.

The wolves had fallen quiet. I wondered if I'd imagined their cries rising with mine.

"Now, do I tell you about your brother again?" I said to him, not looking at him.

"Forget it," he said. "You're frecking crazy, Jezebel. Whatever you told me would be a pile of crap."

I felt drowsy, but it was a thin skin over my unease, my dread. Was this another snare? What's he playing for? Tell me the truth. No, any truth you tell will be a lie.

"If," I said, "you're not going to execute me, or hand me over to a madhouse somewhere, or even listen to what I say, or even credit what I say, why don't you get out and go to hell?"

"Maybe I will," he said. It's the mumble, lazy, indifferent.

I sat daintily drinking blood that tasted of fruit, and he sat, but I didn't look at him, didn't know what he did, his presence like red-hot metal a few feet away over my shoulder. I thought I'd become his experiment. In the morning, perhaps, he'd dissect me.

For sure, he wouldn't sleep. Watch and prey.

Like a picture of an invalid, I lay on my bed, propped up high, the glass of nourishment to hand, covered by a paper cloth. He didn't try to prevent me from coming back here, just watched me. I shut the window and pulled the blind and now the sixty-second dawn was beginning and the blind was a shining sapphire.

The juice wasn't enough, not really enough, to restore me after my dose of golden radiation. And besides, it wouldn't last long.

I'd tried to think of a way out of this. I'd tried to imagine some way I could appease him. But I didn't think he really knew anymore what he wanted from me. Maybe in the end he'd come up the stairs and beat me and rape me, and then he'd go away. Or maybe he'd just go.

Or maybe he wouldn't.

The day was overcast, the sky a gray-pink almond fondant. It was the kind of day I could go out on, the kind of day I used to wait for and use, for here, in the revitalized atmosphere of Novo Mars, that kind of overcast, once formed, remained till sundown.

Had the wind changed? I mean, the wind of ill-fortune.

I decided to display normalcy, what normalcy I could. I rose and showered. The shower was temperamental, being accustomed to my touch, because another had used it, and now it hesitated to respond to me, the hot too hot, and the cold too cold. I put on some of my black clothes, I brushed my hair, and fixed my face before the mirror. Then, on impulse, I brought my single traveling bag from under the bed, and packed it as if I were planning another trip, and when I'd stored the bag again, under the bed, I hung my black straw hat ready on the mirror. It was a premonition. Like the premonition I felt on the air-bug, going to Ares for Cassi's funeral, like the premonition I had the night I visited my mother's grave: foretastes of Death the hunter.

I walked downstairs, and I heard a sound thwack on the dry ground. The glass door stood open on the sugar almond day, and Jace was framed in the door and the day, twenty feet away along the slope. He was digging a grave for all the bits of his brother's bones. I glanced at the door, automatic and forewarned, since he wouldn't have gone outside without arranging the door. The lectro-chain was shorted, the self-lock quietly broken from inside, and bent.

A day like this, I didn't even need sunglasses. I could take in horizons, even the road, and a filmy high-speed dot of car. I stood on the porch, and looked at Jace working with the shovel. I felt a little twist of reassurance standing there in the safe morning. His face was all shut up and with its blinds down, unreadable, the way my face becomes when something is tearing at me. I wondered if he were torn. Of course he was. Why else his advent here and the cruel tricks of vengeance, undecided and malevolent as any of Hamlet's.

Around the other side of the house, by the pump which had excavated Sand, and which provided my mother's ghost with something fresh to stare at, Sand's bones had lain all yesterday and all yesterday night. Now they were in a neat indecipherable pile by the hole Jace was digging. It didn't have to be a large hole. It was already large enough.

Then Jace Vincent shocked me. Into the carefully dug, only ethically necessary grave he kicked, systematically and sparsely, the bones of his dead.

I went down the steps and crossed over to him and watched him cover them with dusts and soil.

"A ministering angel shall thy brother be," I said to Jace, "when I lie howling."

He tamped the soil flat, and let the spade go. He looked at me, and I beheld I had not reached him at any time, nor in any way. I had not even scratched the surface of what he was.

That second, the real fear caught up to me, the worse-than-fear. I had been trying to assess him by what I'd learned of men, and suddenly I saw none of these clues applied. He wasn't any kind, but neither was he of any kind I knew, and an overcast, a bag under a bed, a glass of red juice, were not sufficient talismans.

And then we both heard the high-speed car's rolling roar as it skimmed off the road onto the track.

"Who are you expecting?" Jace asked me.

I didn't say anything.

In a dust ball, the vehicle whirled toward us, already slowing on big silent brakes. As the fumes soaked down on the air, the size of the car became obvious. It was a four-seater auto-drive, the color of old copper, which rejected the dust that tried to settle on it as it overshot the track, and came to rest ten feet away. The polarized one-way windows were blanks. Then the side door lifted. Out climbed Cassi's executor, my uncle-in-law, Hog Koberman.

The Hog stared at once at Jace. Clearly, I'd guessed wrong before; they'd never met. The Hog didn't recognize Jace, but the Hog's features, his whole stance, implied disapproval, and uneasiness. This was to have been the Hog's party.

Then his eyes slid away from Jace, who presumably was impenetrably and intractably undiminished. The Hog's eyes lit instead on the spot of new-turned soil, and the fallen spade.

I can shriek: Uncle, save me from this madman who insists I killed his brother, the bones of said brother having just been buried where your eye is riveted. Jace can say: A woman who feeds dead men in her incinerator needs treatment. Neither of us is likely to say such things. I don't want trouble and incrimination, I don't want a planet-state institution any more than I want to die. And Jace, for whatever reason, doesn't want to surrender me to anyone else.

"Another burial, Bella?" the Hog asked me, with obscene accuracy and surprising lack of social taste.

Jace is silent, letting me make the first move, waiting for the cat to jump.

In a second or so, the Hog will also note the demolished lock fitments on the porch door.

"A thief broke in the house," I said, "while I was in town. He didn't take much, my dog scared him off." It's mostly the same story I attempted before. "But he killed the dog."

"Good God, Bel," said uncle, "this should be reported to the police." He risked a man-to-man antagonistic glare at Jace. "And who are you?"

Jace said, "Ask the lady, she'll tell you."

Confused, frustrated, the Hog swung to me.

"A neighbor. He helped me, with the dog."

"Jason," Jace said. "Name's Jason." He smiled at

the Hog suddenly, a snow-white smile of parochial gregariousness that threw the Hog off-balance instantly.

"Well then," the Hog said. He came to me and took my arm, angling us away from Jace. "Shall we go into the house?"

"All right."

We walked. Jace, naturally, came after us, sticking to us with a modest, eager-to-please doggedness. Uncle tried to ignore this dark and golden beast upon our trail.

At the door, uncle examined the two loose tongues of the lock.

"The police, Bella. You contacted them?

"Yes, of course."

"What are they doing?"

"Looking. . . ."

The Hog was satisfied but omnipotent.

"If you have any trouble—"

"Thank you."

"Strange I should drop by right now," he said. (Stranger than you think.) "I had some business out Brade way, and took a notion to drive over into this Styx of yours. I have the bimonthly figures of your investment program. There's also another matter—"

But really, it's just curiosity, uncle. You just wanted to see where I am, what I'm doing, the strange weeping girl in sunglasses, the social outcast of the tribe. Maybe you fancy me, too, your arm constantly around my shoulders, your hand on my arm, your breathing in my face. Whatever it is, you're here.

In the hall we paused.

"That's a fine window above the stairs, Bel."

Last night, this hall was an arena of the most basic savagery, of my screaming desperation. of Jace's blackness rising from the dark. My mother died out here. Now this stupid man stands and admires the damn window.

We went into the parlor. Uncle sat.

"I wonder if you have any iced tea?" wondered uncle.

Glibly, against my earlier statement, I said, "The thief took everything from my cupboards and my freezer."

"All she can offer you is water," added Jace obligingly from the doorway. He leaned there, shutting us in.

Unless you care for a drop of blood?

I laughed noiselessly and snapped the laugh off my face. Jason Vincent watched me. Uncle didn't see. Uncle was alone with two of the most dangerous creatures he was ever likely to mix with. Stop it, Sabella. Whatever you do, you mustn't feel part of a conspiracy with Jace; condemned and executioner aren't coupled in a primitive rite.

"Oh," said Hog Koberman, "Mr. Jason—pardon me, but there are some private matters I should like to discuss with Bella here."

Jace smiled accommodatingly. He would do uncle a favor and not mind. But he wouldn't move.

"Bel—" uncle said to me. I didn't offer a solution. The Hog made a wrong judgment he should wrongly have made some while before. His face engaged with his distaste, his disappointment. "Very well. If that's the way you want it, Bella."

"*Sa*bella," I said. I don't really know why.

Uncle's head jerked. "Excuse me?"

"*Sa*bella," I said. "That's my name." I looked at Jace. "*Sabella*."

Uncle became very formal. Very proper.

"If you prefer. Sabella. Before we come to the investment figures, Sabella—"

"How about," Jace said, "Miss Quey."

Uncle jumped. He looked at Jace, and at me.

"Sabella—"

"Miss Quey," said Jace, "Spelled Q-U-E-Y. Pronounced Kay. Try it."

Hog Koberman was speechless. He looked at me, waiting for rescue, and then he stood up.

"I'd hoped to deal with this personally, Sabella." Nervously, involuntarily, he hesitated for Jace's interpolation, but none came. "Now I see a letter would be more in the order of things."

Jace stood aside from the door graciously, making way for Hog Koberman to pass through. Jace wanted to drive the visitor off, and he'd succeeded, the visitor was leaving.

Suddenly, a chasm split in front of us. The decision was so swift there was no space for doubt or conjecture.

I strolled quietly past Jace, and after the Hog, and I caught the Hog at the porch.

"I'll walk you to your car," I said.

"There's no need."

"I'd like to."

"Very well, Sabella."

We went out again. I took uncle's pudgy arm. Jace followed, slow, a guard hound pacing us, fifteen feet behind.

"Now," I said, "tell me what you wanted to say."

"What I *wanted* to say hardly comes into it, Bel—Sabella. I have a mystery on my hands, and I was in hopes you might throw some light on it."

I was barely listening.

"Yes, whatever you think."

"It's this business of old John Trim's death."

We were marching toward the big car, Uncle dragging me by my hand on his arm which he wouldn't acknowledge and I wouldn't release. When he said, "Old John Trim," it was like a record tape, snagged and repeating. I'd heard it before, yet it was meaningless.

"You understand, Bella—Sabella, I have responsibilities to the Koberman estate. After John's death I was sent certain documents of his. I learned from these that Cassilda had made Trim a private antemortem payment, which had at no time been declared for tax. A foolish illegality for Cassilda to have committed. On top of it, John was being harassed for money by some person who seems to have made a lucky guess about the payment. A term of detention at Trim's age would have finished him. In fact, the threat was enough. His stroke was doubtless due to worry at the harassment he was receiving. Among his effects was an unmailed letter, intended for the vulture who was threatening him, containing an enclosure of credit bonds. There was also evidence of the previous relationship of the two concerned. The reason I trouble you with the affair, Bella, is that apparently Trim had hired the man in the first instance at your aunt's instigation, in the capacity of a private investigator, the subject of the investigation being yourself."

We're all mad. The Hog's mad too.

Sand, a blackmailer, my gentle-voiced, sweet and sunlit lover?

Uncle was waiting for my reply, so I replied, but not verbally. I punched him in the stomach, a blow of such force he never could have reckoned my little white-knuckled fist would inflict it. And as he bent, choking, I threw myself past him into the car. Anyone can operate auto-drive.

The door sizzled down, and through the one-way window I had a final glimpse of uncle kneeling on the ground, his head in the dust. Behind him, Jace, running, but a fat hog in the way.

Then the car spun itself about, as Sand's car did just over two months ago. It raced for the road below. These big custom-built chariots, they do a maximum of two hundred, faster than most traffic there is. Jace's car, small enough to be parked out of sight, wouldn't have a speed like this.

The packed bag was only a symbol, and the hat for traveling.

I've left it all behind. And I've left another enemy, another witness for my prosecution.

"Say good-bye," Jace said, when he smashed the glass container. Now I've said good-bye to everything.

When I got near the Brade Highway, Route 09, I took the bills I found in Hog Koberman's wallet compartment. The credit cards I didn't dare to touch, not from honesty, but because card-users could be traced in minutes by the central computer of the banking system. That the Hog carried bills at all surprised me, as Jace's possession of bills had. I suppose they were a rich man's small-change, and for Jace, a good-faith token to the blonde whore he had brought that night to the house. I didn't feel compunction at robbery. In a world of enemies, compunction is a flaw no survivor could indulge. I'd stolen lives, after all. Cash was nothing.

After I'd pocketed the bills, I stopped the car. There was nothing on the road, either way. I got out, jammed on the accelerator, manually slammed down the door, and watched the vehicle plow on up the highway. A top-speeder has a built-in avoidance pattern to miss other traffic, halt at obstacles or roadblocks, or pedestrians. Meeting none of those, it will run until its solar cells dry out. With luck, the police uncle would undoubtedly alert wouldn't realize that the blank windows hid an empty space.

I walked into Brade Corner in ten minutes. The Corner is one of fifty outposts of Brade itself. People come and go constantly, and no one remembers faces. In a dim little underground parlor I let someone quick-set my hair with a haphazard bleaching that would fade in streaks—I could refine it later. Somewhere else again, I bought a red dress and a large red bag, and somewhere suntan makeup for girls who come in from the cold planets. Then I took a cab to Brade lift-off point.

It was thirteen o'clock, unlucky thirteen, when I boarded the air-bug to Ares.

Who'd reckon I'd head for Ares, Koberman country? But Ares is like all big cities, like the Plateau, a wide tract of land where names don't matter, but the hunting is good by night.

I suppose I could have run to the hills, but years of human comforts had softened me. I couldn't live in a cave, not now. Besides I'd dreamed of those hills, and Jace Vincent had found me in that dream. Maybe I was just insane as well as full of hate and fear and anger, and tired of making allowances, cheating myself. Saying no, Sabella, no.

I sat in my bright bloody dress, and I looked around the plane, and the dull sky shone in the windows. I didn't care any more, you see. I'd tried, and my reward was punishment. I wouldn't try anymore.

The name on my ticket was Sarah Holland. Sarah was my mother's name, and Holland was the promotion name on a long billboard advertising bottled water as the Hog's car burned through Canyon.

Sarah Holland doesn't care about cold fanatical Cassi, or shifty shifting Sand that Sabella had taken, scorched in her own horror and guilt, while he had been trying all along to take her too, and Trim, and how many others, perhaps, back in his insecure, faltering father-brother-haunted-past.

Even Jace has no part in Sarah's world.

When Sarah was fourteen, she went with a boy in a car. And when she was sixteen, seventeen, eighteen, she went with all the boys. Her mother never said to her, "Sarah, what are doing to yourself?" Sarah's mother hadn't cared.

Sarah has no pursuers, and no guilt. Sarah won't let herself tremble with reaction.

Sarah can live with all she is.

Sarah will have to.

Part THREE

De Profundis

1

The nights I don't go out I sit and watch the skies above the city. I mentioned the clouds, and the lights of the city on the clouds, long ago. I explained about the hills of concrete and glass, and the valleys of neon and the trees of blue steel. The subways rumble wild as rivers. Great mountains of apartment blocks stand black on rays of white and indigo and violet. Sometimes jeweled birds fly over, planes coming into the landing strips of the port, or the golden tail of a phoenix, a space ship taking a fix on our glow, heading in to some point a thousand miles away.

In the end, maybe, I'll go off-planet. Maybe I should go to Earth. But the hills are green and the skies are blue, how strange, how oppressive. I think I could only go to Earth to die.

I move about a lot, anyway, a month here, a month there. Five days in Cliffton, ten in Iles, three in Dale.

My hair's pure blonde tinsel, but I have a wig which is black, woven of darkness. I wear white frocks and red, and stockings with silver seams. Guess what I do, nights?

I haven't killed yet. The whole Christawful city is riddled with men who are searching for me, the whore who gave them the lay of their life, but they can't recall why. I charge them cash, too, since I have to pay the rent somehow. Sometimes I even meet one of my customers again. I never say no. But then I move on again, and they're safe, till next time.

Did I say I never say "no"? Once I did. In a bar behind the spin-drive stadium. He was a racer and he came up to me. Jet black hair and golden skin. He reminded me of Jace.

"Come on, honey," he said. "Why not?"

Those fine black ink-and-brush-painted hairs were on his hands, lean and articulate with handling the blazing wheel of the spin-track. Had Jace done that, too? What had Jace done in any event, that I know of? Except hunt for me. Was he still hunting? Was the pig-man helping him now?"

"I don't do it with spin-racers."

"Yes you do."

"When I do it with a spin-racer, he crashes."

They have superstition on the track. As he got up and left me, I caught the glimmer of a gold cross on his gold skin.

I left Cassi's cross in the house, and the casket, and everything else.

I missed the house. The colored window, the deck of music, the wolves' music in the loudly silent nights.

An overcast day—the cities are richer in these, pale-blue oxygen overcast on lavender—I went out. I saw a tinstone C.R. mission, the House of the Shepherd. New and shiny, with a great white banner. The banner said: WHAT ARE YOU LIVING FOR? LIVE FOR JESUS.

It's been three months since I ran. Five months since Sand was burned to bones.

Sometimes it seems odd that they haven't traced me after all. Other times, I know they never will.

So what am I living for? For what happens when I take? I'll tell you something, when I take, now, nothing happens to me. It's a hunger and I feed it. Like sex to some of them, an itch to scratch. Not like breathing anymore. Each time I hunt on the slopes of concrete, through the ravines of metal brick, my excitement says to me, this time it will be special, like it was. Why isn't it? And if it isn't, why do I go on? Perhaps it is a drug, a habit, and I could break it. Perhaps I'm deranged, need help. Put me in a doll's house, lock me away. I'm preying on your city, sinking teeth in it, sucking its veins.

The pendant blazes. It's a ruby and never less than a ruby, and some nights it's a dragon's eye.

Before I became Sarah my life was just a series of roles. My mother's daughter, a hundred men's dream-lay, Sand's oyster, Jace's Hamlet-vengeance, Cassi's scapegoat. When was I ever my own?

Now I'm Sarah, I drink the air (which has become the mud). Now I'm truly me. But no, Sabella. Now I belong entirely to the blood-red stone around my neck.

Maybe, indirectly, Cassi's plan to destroy me is working after all.

Meantime, I watched the skies above the city.

There are about ten churches in Ares. Ten churches to around ten thousand bars, around ten thousand girl-houses, twenty-seven landing strips, fifteen spin-drive stadiums, twenty-five cinemats, ninety public swim pools, nine hundred hyper-markets, eight hundred automats, six hundred lavatories.

But once there were no churches at all. Till the Revivalists built them. Silver tinstone and white plasti-plaster, blue concrete, stained glass. Spires like metal pylons with crosses that light up by night.

I hadn't been in church for around eleven years, apart from Cassi's chapel, and the chapel at Angel Meadow when momma died. Sarah Holland had never been in church at all, nor did I suppose she'd have any hankering to be.

Of the ten or so, about half stay open at night, and the utensils on the altar have faintly glowing lectro devices around them.

I'd been hunting and I'd taken, and I was going home to where home was just then, which was an apartment block on Eighteenth Dale. The cross of the church, like an emerald badge pinned on the night, appeared between the tall stacks and crags of the buildings, and then the pale wall, and then the wide-open doorway. I hadn't seen this place previously, though others like it many times. The warm-tinted soft light inside, the musty incense smell. Above the door was a treated painted panel. This Christ looked like Sand Vincent, the longish dark hair, dark eyes, amber flesh.

Before I knew it, Sarah Holland walked up the steps in at the door.

I sat on one of the polished benches, and looked at the altar. The cloth was dark red, embroidered with green and gold, the Cloth of the Blood of the Redeemer. A mutedly lit sign gave the times of the services, which were all done for tonight. No one was there but me; so I sat, my spine pressed against the hard supporting plank of the bench. I wondered why I was there, but the church was quiet. The peace was heavy on the air as any scent.

Then a priest came out of the back and began to walk along the aisle.

I meant to get up and go out at once, but my feet were heavy, had grown into the floor, I was weighted down on the bench. I stared straight ahead, but, of course, the priest would come to me. Presently he spoke.

"Can I help you in any way?"

His voice was young, younger than he'd looked coming toward me.

"No, thank you very much."

"Are you sure?"

I should never have come in here.

"Yes, I'm sure. I just wanted to sit for a while."

I know he's taking in my garb and my hair.

"Christ can help you," the priest said, "even if you won't let me."

I turned and stared hard at him, and I said, "If He knows the things I've called Him, He won't help."

The priest startled me by smiling. "Oh, I think He'd understand about that."

He was trying to draw me out, gently and kindly. And I felt the danger of a response. For three months I'd only really spoken to those I meant to have. And what was this? Childhood's theology hanging on my shoulder.

"Look," I said, "I won't discuss Jesus Christ with you."

"No," he said, "you don't have to discuss Him with anyone."

"You don't mind if I sit here."

"I'm glad for you to, if it helps."

Does it?

I wish I could tell him the truth and he'd pray with me and Christ would come down like a dove on the altar and make it all right.

The priest moved on and left me alone, but my own emotional prodigality had driven off the mood of peace from me, leaving me in the midst of the peace, in a little vacuum of dread and confusion.

You thought I was happy, did you, the wolf-bitch stalking the city?

I walked home to my unhome on Eighteenth Dale. I had a dream that night. I dreamed I was wandering through the house at Hammerhead. But the house was very old, ruinous and piled with pink rusting dusts of the desert. The blinds were torn and the doors broken and even the indestructible glass of the windows was cracked. In my bedroom, the bed was just a frame, and dust webs hung from the carved posts instead of gauze curtains. Then I came to the mirror and I saw myself. I wore the black night-hair wig I wore in the church, but it was thick with blood, and ends spiked stiff with it. There was blood over my mouth and down my dress (the way there'd been blood on my dress the first time, when I was fourteen, my own blood and the boy's). My nails were long and pointed and sheathed in blood. My eyeballs were scarlet. My lips were parted and I saw my teeth were very long, like white needles; and my tongue was a thin black whip. The terror that filled me was unspeakable, unutterable. And when I plunged awake, the terror was still with me, clamped inside me, a tumor on my invisible, shadow-casting, mirror-image-making, nonexistent soul.

The next sunset, I went back to the church. I went back without the black wig, in another dress, hoping the priest wouldn't recognize me. It was between services, and the church had emptied, all but for one woman kneeling, and the priest at the altar, who didn't seem to see me at all. Then there was another woman kneeling, and it was me.

You look like Sand, and I don't believe in you, or if I do, I resist the belief. I've cursed you and profaned you, and I'll do it again. I've never served you and I never will. Every minute that I'm not afraid I'll forget you. I can't make a bargain. But help me, help me. Help me, if you can, or you're there, or if anyone's there, or no one. Help me. Help me.

Then I went home to Eighteenth Dale. I brought a bottle of pills from the pharmacy across the way. But I only took five, and then I got sick, and it wasn't any use.

Next morning, the Ares sky was overcast, and my rent was up at Eighteenth Dale. I packed my red bag that I bought at Brade Corner with the things I bought at Cliffton when I arrived in the big city. It was time to move on.

I moved into a room at Iles, and I went with a blond spacer. His blood had been purified by the stars of space, but it was still mud, and I still had to have it. I also had to get out in the dark. He couldn't leave me alone, nor I resist his entreaties, and I was coming perilously close to killing him. At one in the morning I panicked, and when he was unconscious I smeared the jel on his neck and I ran.

I ran straight for the church in Dale.

The altar cloth was white and blue and I couldn't remember why. I huddled into the pew-bench and laid my head on the rail of the bench in front. I didn't know what I was doing there. If the priest had come out I would have bolted, but there was only a man near the door in the shadow, head on hands, praying.

And then I turned and looked, and he wasn't praying, and it was Jace.

I got up slowly, and slowly returned to the door, and he didn't react. Then I got outside, and he was there, and he caught my arm.

The touch of his hand on my arm, my skin, stopped me.

"How?" was the only word I could get out.

His voice was so familiar, I must have been hearing it in my sleep.

"You have religion," he said. "It was just a matter of when and where."

"Let me go," I said.

He said, ignoring that, "I've been to every goddamned church in Ares. I left a call code. I told them I was looking for my sister."

"*Sister?*"

The priest, the kind priest, wanting to be kind. Any woman can bleach her hair, wear a white dress. When I was praying to Jesus for help, the priest was looking at me, recognizing me despite blonde hair, black hair, from Jace's description. When I was vomiting up the pills, the priest was calling Jace.

I'm immobile in his grasp, except I'm shivering in the hot city night.

"Still want to kill me for Sand? Sand, the blackmailer, the cheat."

"I know what Sand was," Jace said.

"He looked like Christ over the door."

"Sure he did. That was his big number. Extortion, blackmail, those weren't new games for Sand. He raped a girl on Gall Vulcan. You find that hard to believe? So did she, till he did it to her. And I was the insurance, the demon brother who had to clean up whenever the stuff hit the fan, which it always did."

"So why come after me?"

"To see how far he'd implicated me this time, and in what. Whatever you and he had been into. He did write me. That was part of the fun, to show me what a great deal he was making for himself. Only the deals stank, and they never came off. Then I'd get the stella from the belly of the whale: Get me out, Jace. No stella at all was special. After what he'd said about you, it sounded as if the pot had boiled over. I'd say he meant to take you for everything you had, but then you did your magic act on him, and he shot for Trim instead. Someone was bound to get Sand one day. It just happened to be you."

I recalled Sand's confession, and his trying to run away from me across the desert, when he was dying, afraid I must be paying him out for discovered tricks. I recalled Jace's profile, yellowing, when Sand's bones landed in the dust.

"This is another trap," I said.

"Whatever it is, you're stuck with it."

"Does Koberman know?"

"The fat man? No. This is a private war, Sabella."

"Cozy-cozy," I said. My teeth chattered, as Sand's teeth chattered when I tried to drive him to the hospital. "But Koberman will still be looking for me."

"I doubt it."

His tone was unequivocal. He'd obviously warned the Hog away, perhaps merely by threats of violence. Jace *is* violence, or at least, violent power. I should know. I was held in the vise of it.

"Stop shaking," he said, "I'm not going to hurt you."

"Because you hated your kiddy brother after all."

I'd tried to kill myself. If Jace killed me, it would settle everything. Apparently, I was not a survivor anymore. Even Sarah wasn't.

"I didn't hate him. You don't hate the garbage."

"The great Daniel would be proud of you."

"Daniel," he said, so soft I nearly missed it.

"Your father. You forgot? Your golden marvel god of a father that Sand worshiped, second only to you. Your family has a truly biblical ambience, the Patriarch and his two sons. One with the mark of Cain on his forehead."

"You're the lady with the incinerator," he said, "and the sick dog."

"And you still don't know how he died, or why." I paused. I watched the neons making flaming smoke of the clouds. "I'll show you."

"O.K.," he said.

He turned me unexpectedly toward him, and our eyes met, and I thought of the dream of the deer and the hills and the man with the gun, and I leered at him, and in my imagination my teeth were long as daggers."

"You've made a mess of yourself," he said to me. "Your hair, the way you've dyed your skin. You look as though you've slept hanging on a peg."

"Now I really want you to see," I said to him. "I want you to see what I did to Sand."

I knew I was insane, but I couldn't pull myself up. I'd raced to the brink, and leapt, and I was dropping through the air and I couldn't save myself if I tried. I was even exhilarated, horribly excited. I did want him to see. I did want him to know. An ultimate witness, to condemn me. As my mother was the first.

"Come on," I said. "We walk."

He shifted his grip to my elbow, and we did walk, down the steps of the church, under the reflected glory of the emerald cross.

There was a bar three blocks away; I'd been there before. Someone would be loitering, looking for a girl. There always was someone.

We walked without speaking, but at the street, where you could see the bar's bright sheen and three men leaning on the wall outside, smoking, I said to Jace, "Now for the demonstration. Let go my arm and watch."

His grip came off me immediately and for a moment I felt disoriented, adrift. How could he trust me? Could he read me so well he knew on this occasion I was on the level? Then I was walking on. I went toward the three men, and they looked, and I smiled.

"Hey, girlie," they said.

They reached for me. The one I wanted was in the

middle, the youngest, the most tender shoot. "Last dance tonight," I said. And I put out my hand, and the young one took my hand.

The other two laughed and congratulated us, and the boy and I came back up the street, past Jace, and Jace fell in behind us.

"Who's he? said the boy.

"My protector," I said. "Don't worry."

"Who's worried," said the boy, "but most of you girls are free lance. In case you have any ideas—" he revealed a switchblade, the old kind with the razor welded to the outer edge. This boy was younger than Sand. But then, Sand wasn't innocent either. I've taken so many and thought of them as victims, but maybe I'm the victim.

"You don't get it," I said to the boy with the razor switch. "If you let him watch, you needn't pay."

"Oh really?" The boy grinned. He grinned back at Jace. "Be my guest, mister." He's stupid. He's perfect.

A loading alley for robot carts ran between high steel walls. I led the boy, and we stepped over the rails, and Jace came behind.

"Here?" I asked.

"Freck it," said the boy. "I thought you had a bed."

"Come on," I said. "Who needs beds?"

He acquiesced and slid his hands up under my skirt and I released the sealer on his pants.

I didn't have any need, not really, and I was in complete control. Jace was standing a few yards off, black on black shadow, as in the dream.

I didn't feel pity anymore. Or a desire to give pleasure in return. I hated this boy working away in me, squeezing me, grinding me back against the metal wall. I called softly to Jace, "Now watch me, honey." The boy grunted his breathless contempt. I kissed his neck. He tasted of smoke and alcohol and darkness and sex. In the dimness, I wondered if Jace would see. Somehow, I knew he would. I was touching the vein, and the boy groaned. I was in control, but I bit hard and deep, almost carelessly. The boy yelped and then he reared against me, trying to thrust himself through me into the wall.

I took very little, then I let him go, and he fell away from me and on his face beside the rails.

I pulled my clothes straight automatically, practiced.

"Come and see, Jason," I said.

He came toward me, and I was going to tell him what to look for when he leaned over the boy, grasped his loose head by the hair, and examined the throat. There was more blood than usual, and the wound was glaring black in the dimness.

"That's what I did to Sand," I said. "And he loved it. He begged for it. I tried to save his life when it was too late. But there are plenty I didn't. I'm a lady with a past all littered with dead young gentleman callers."

Then I went by Jace and rubbed the heal-fast coagulant jel into the wound. When I'd finished, I straightened and Jace took my elbow and we walked away.

I looked up at his face. Unreadable.

"You do understand," I said. I looked unreadable too.

He didn't answer.

"I drink blood. I need to. The juice in the container was blood. Does it surprise you a vampire has religion?" I couldn't stop talking, and he apparently couldn't start. "It shouldn't surprise you. Jesus Christ, after all, was a vampire. Oh, yes, Jason, Jesus was a vampire. They drank blood at the last supper, and then the priests impaled him on a stake of wood. To be sure, they drove a wooden stake in his side. God made the sky go black by day out of pity for Jesus's agony in the sunlight. When he was dead, they buried him, but he resurrected, the way a vampire is supposed to. You can't keep a good man down."

See, Jesus? You wouldn't help me, so now I'm blaspheming you for all I'm worth. When I'm in hell, you can come and stoke the fires.

We'd crossed suddenly out onto one of the broad lit-up bridges of the Dale-Iles thoroughfare. A hundred feet below, an empty walkway, and traffic gushing on thirty-two lanes, like streaks of fire, a river of multicolored lavas. And all around, the distant volcanoes and the mountains rose in impersonal waterfalls of neon.

"All you have to do," I said to Jace, "is lift me up over the rail and let me fall on the walkway. They threw Jezebel out of a window."

Jace had let go of me again. He rested his forearms on the rail of the bridge. The streaks of car-fire burned across his eyes. He was alone. I wasn't with him anymore.

"All right," I said. "I suppose you'll tell someone, sometime. Here's my address: four on twenty-sixth, Iles. The name on the tag is Sarah Holland. I'll wait for you, or who you send. Remember, every night you delay, I'll be out here, busy."

My head was up to look at him, and the wind, full of sparks and spirits of electricity and oxygen, blew back my cold-color hair. Then he turned his head and his eyes glared down at me, hard black surfaces, showing me what he saw. I'm dirt. I'm cheap and demented and filthy. He saw that. You don't hate the garbage.

I turned my back and walked on.

When they put me into the hospital they may cure me. Or if they don't I'll die.

But if my courage fails me, I'll just move out of four on twenty-sixth, Iles, and the circus will continue. I can keep away from churches now.

He found me. What was the point if it goes nowhere?

I hadn't wanted him to kill me. I'd wanted him to say to me it would be all right. Not a dove on an altar, but Jace. Not prayer, but Jace. Not Jesus.

Jace.

A mail chute slanted up into my room at four on twenty-sixth. A couple of random circulars came along the chute in the morning when I was drearily, restlessly sleeping. The package came later, and woke me from a nightmare like a grave. Awake, the grave persisted, since I knew what the package was. It was my haunting, Cassi's casket.

I opened the package, and I lifted out the casket. It was rather funny, had an element of burlesque, the way three times I'd been given this thing. There was the sinister quality, too. This version of the casting of runes. I knew who'd sent it now, delivered it by hand through the chute marked four, twenty-six *Holland*, ten stories down. But there was a miniature self-play tape in with the casket.

For half an hour, I couldn't make myself press the button to activate the tape. Maybe I never would have, but part of me, a very shamed foolish part, wanted to hear his voice, whatever it said to me. And this small part finally pressed in the button.

"Your friend, the Hammerhead mailman, hung onto the parcel with Cassi Koberman's box in it. Your recent life seems full of those of us trying to test which side of the law you walk. The mailman thought he could play games and you wouldn't report him. Then he sobered up some, and got scared you might. I know, because I had a couple of drinks with the bastard, the day before I took the box off him. I've talked with a few people about you Sabella. Don't backtrack on that. None of them can get near you, or has the guts to try. As for Cassi's box, I guess you couldn't have opened it the second time. When the fat man left, I went through your house on the Plateau, and I found the box, and opened it. Trim John sent it to you, just before he died. He put his own letter in the box. You haven't read the letter. Read it."

The voice ended there, and I paced about waiting for more, but the blank tail of the tape coiled on, with nothing, and then stopped.

I thought of Jace's eyes, on the bridge. The voice was unchanged, the lazy slurred drawl, even an edge of bevelled humor on the "*Trim* John." I thought of other things after that, but finally I set the key in the casket and lifted the lid, and took out the sheet of fine quality paper—finer than the paper Cassi's curse had been written on.

I expected to be cursed again. I spent a while looking at the thin, spidery, stilted writing, so I wouldn't have to read the words. "Miss Sabella Quey," it began. "Miss Sabella Quey, When Mrs. Koberman went to Easterly and came home with the warmth of God Almighty in her heart, I was glad for her. But then she had this notion that God's angels had warned her against you. And all her last days, she was planning how she would get to you through the law, because she said that they don't burn witches, and the law was the only recourse she had. To begin with, she provided you a sum in her will. She believed the chance of the money would ensure your presence at her funeral, while, if you had vacated the house at Hammerhead, a newscast announcement was to be made of your mention in the will, similarly intended to draw you from seclusion. Next, she selected a young man, a private investigator in Dawson, and instructed me to hire him. She had seen from the advertisement that the young man's name was Sand Vincent, and insisted that, because of his name, she understood God had selected him to carry on His work against you. Well then, Miss Quey, Mrs. Koberman died, and I did what she'd told me because you get accustomed to obeying a woman you've obeyed for ten-odd years. But Mr. Vincent isn't God's agent, Mr. Vincent is an evil man. The day after we put Mrs. Koberman to rest Mr. Vincent came back to the house for his rented car, which he had parked beside the cemetery. He told me he was driving out west to Hammerhead Plateau, to see you, Miss Quey. He said he had things arranged between you and everything was going as he wished. But then he threatened me over a certain payment that Mrs. Koberman had made to me. This evil boy is from the devil, and has not done with me, or with any of us. You see, Miss Quey, not being well, I can write these things, but I should be quick. I think that your aunt was led falsely in her supposings. I think that, rather than to chastise you, she was meant to bring you to salvation. It's a wonderful thing to approach God, and His Only True Son, Jesus Christ, whose love emcompasses all worlds and states and times. If you could know the comfort it brings me, even in my agitation, I believe you, too, would turn to Him. And for this reason, I advise you to go to Easterly, Miss Quey. It was there that Cassilda Koberman found her faith and there she learned what she upheld to be this bad thing which you had done, though she never confided in me as to what this thing might be. In Easterly there's a church, and here is where she said she was directed to discover this terrible thing. Or maybe we have all been mistaken. But I felt obliged to reveal all these matters to you, in hopes you also will seek redemption. And I ask you to forgive me if I have wronged you. I remain, most faithfully yours, John Michael Trim."

The extraordinary form of this letter. It's religious fever coupled to its curious formality; its blindness, its doubts, its pedantry, its childishness, linked to the stoicism with which John Trim recognized oncoming sudden death.

I visualized again his frail hands on the stair rail, his impartial, self-effacing solemnity. (Can I recall his face?)

But none of that took me nearer to any point of reference. So I reread the letter. John Trim advised me to go back to Easterly for the salvation of my soul. An old man's naïve fanatical deed of expiation. But why had Jace augmented it?

I pulled the blind of polarized glass over the window, for the day was burning bright. Easterly. Already I could smell the aniseed grass, see the cotton wool over the refinery chimneys. Already I could feel momma as she slapped my fourteen-year-old face in my locked bedroom, and hear the sound of men marshaling for a wildcat hunt, and the noise the wind makes, blowing over the river, the meadows, and the dry canals. And by the hole in the rock where I found my pendant.

Easterly's where it started. Maybe it had to end there.

I read Trim's letter yet again. 'Why did the name Sand Vincent make Cassi judge him suitable to her scheme?) Then I played the tape again, but all I heard was Jace's voice, not what he said.

He stood in the dark, and watched me with the boy from the bar. Jace watched me, and then he examined the boy, and then he walked with me, and he never spoke. "I drink blood," I said to him. Only the second time I ever vocalized it. The first time, momma hit me and yelled at me. He didn't answer. He didn't hit me, or yell, or laugh, or try to reason with or kill me. As if—

As if he'd been expecting it all. As if he knew.

I know what you are, Sabella. I didn't know until I came to God, but when I found God, He told me. I hope the cross cripples you, as it should. You're just one of the wolves.

His angels told me. I know what you've done.

Cassi had found God at Easterly, and her heart should have exploded with love, but instead she went crusading, and I was the Infidel and she knew it—

And Jace knew it.

How?

It was more than Cassi digesting my mother's old letters, those hints and evasions. It was more than Jace talking to a few people who mistrust me, and guessing. The kind of thing he'd never guess would be a thing like a girl who lives by drinking blood. I doubt if he actually believes it, even now. But he knew it.

It was at Easterly, whatever the truth was.

And then I realized that Jace has had the time, between when he opened the casket and when he waited for me on the off-chance in the church at Dale. He'd had three months since I ran from Hammerhead Plateau. Whatever was at Easterly, he'd been there, and *that was* how he knew.

But the dead are always in league against me. Momma, Cassi, Sand, John Michael Trim. And those others, Frank and Angelo and Benny and Lek and. . . .

Maybe all the dead were sending me to Easterly to die and Jace was the human spokesman for all those ghosts, so real and human and alive that I'd never figure it out until too late.

I sat in the room in Iles, and waited, but no one came to take me into any kind of custody.

So I packed my bag and I went out on the briefly sunset street, and dipped in the minute of fire, an auto-cab came to the walkway. And before the fire had died, I was riding east.

Besides, there was nowhere else to go but Hell.

2

At a car fixit place two miles outside Easterly, having had a moment's forethought, I went into the washroom and slipped on a black dress, took off my silver stockings, combed and pinned my bleached hair into a big knot on my head, and wiped most of the cosmetics off my face. When I was a child there, Easterly had a Puritanical flavor, and being sixty-two miles from Sodom (Ares) had only made it worse. I assume Cassi had gone to visit Easterly again out of nostalgia, and perhaps out of fear. It seems to me she understood death was creeping up on her, and she needed every anchor she could find. So she aimed for her roots, the town she was born in, and with true Koberman luck she caught God and holy war into the bargain. But what do I feel, with only the synthetic tan dye left on my skin, and my sober black dress, do I register anything beyond scents and alarms and old dusts?

It's true, I felt a kind of hankering for Easterly, the way you can look back at childhood, even when it's bitter, longing for all those firsts of life, and those endless wide horizons of unknowledge.

And remembered Easterly, of course, was bigger than I'll ever see it now, and younger, and more important. The brindle oaks, the honeysuckle trees, the children in the streets, the unmechanized bakery that baked real bread; the beer shops and dancing palaces and wicked 3-V cinemats outlawed out of town.

The first thing I saw as the auto-cab decelerated to eighty an hour and cruised in was the great chain of supermarkets built along the highway. And then I saw the surrealistic candy-parlor ballooning over the town, a large striped tent of magenta and white sugar fluorescents.

Everywhere new apartment blocks had been built up like toy bricks, and then spilled over and left lying in the meadows. Automated plants and factories overhung the dam. Where were the refineries? Their chimneys were hidden, like the mines, and only long plumes of smoke, pure bronze on the neonized darkness, flowed up into the night.

There were bars in Easterly, blazing on main street. The novel copper bricks of the ore boom town looked oxidized and pale. The houses crouched between the piles and pylons, a colony invaded by monsters. The old town was being squeezed out like paste from a tube.

Some of the streets were entirely gone to make way for improvements. My street was one of them.

I stopped the cab at the edge, where the half-remembered, half-familiar avenue ended, and where my street, momma's and mine, had begun, and now had ceased to be. It's very odd, the way it just isn't there. As if a chunk of my past had been rubbed out, as if it's only hearsay. Did we really live here? Did any of the events I associate with this spot actually occur? It suddenly seems memory itself could be a fake, come to that. What happened an hour ago, only the fabrication of a mind anxious to possess its background.

Even the trees had vanished.

The times I'd smelled aniseed grass, and thought of this place. And now the one place in my world that I wouldn't smell that grass was here.

I paid off the cab, and it sailed away into the lights and shadows. Then I moved slowly along the concrete sidewalk, through the arches and over the tiled plaza with its fountain of liquid glass. The house would have stood about here. Maybe I would find it. Maybe somewhere it was still here, meshed in the new brickworks and tiles, like those crazy drawings where you win a prize if you can discover the shape of a flower in a girl's eye, or a girl's eye in a flower.

But I didn't win the prize.

Only one thing was sure. The C.R. church had remained. Cassi came to it, and Jace had come to it. John's letter told me that this was where the secret of my sin was blazoned forth for all to see who could read it.

Abruptly my legs were water. I wondered what I was doing here at the whims of my enemies.

Over there, where the apartment blocks stride away beyond the river, a tunnel ran into a quarry. Was that the way I ought to go?

I walked through town, and over the river by a new steel bridge. Then I walked on a new white fluorescent road by the rims of which wild flowers still clustered. My heart roused in my side as I got closer and closer, closer and closer to that afternoon.

About a quarter of a mile from the border of the two dry canals, a wall climbed up into the air. Through an eyelet in the wall, I beheld scaffolding and other walls and a pallid dome which ambiguously might be intended as the future roof of a processing plant or of a theatre. These buildings extended for two or three miles into the night, beyond the point where the quarry had gaped and the hole had gaped in the quarry.

Like vast dunes, they had swarmed over, and smothered it.

I went back to town, and then couldn't remember where the C.R. church was anyway. Subconsciously, no doubt, I had reasons. Consciously, I was simply confused and exhausted. There was a shabby hotel on the corner of one of the older streets. The desk was mechanized, and the lift played tinny music. I went into a room that was like the lift except it had furniture squashed into it. I lay down on the bed and I listened to the noise that Easterly made now, a noise like Ares, but thinner and less sure.

I took ten showers in the closet of that room that night. The room was hot and the windows wouldn't open and the air-conditioning was faulty. I came to imagine there was nobody in the hotel but me, not one human. And I felt alone as I'd never felt alone, alone without even myself for company.

When the sun came and set Easterly on fire, I lay on the bed in the hotel, because it was too bright to go out, too bright and hot to go searching for any answers. But possibly the church would be shut after sundown. I considered waiting for an overcast, but to wait alone in this room and to walk the streets and the dry meadows by night filled me with an obscure fear. I didn't want to take, not in Easterly, where it started. The spacer had been generous, loading me with gifts, and then the boy from the bar had added the last dance of the night. I could hold out two or three nights on that, if I avoided the sun, but one day and night of the allowance were gone, and here was another day.

When the big sun began to wester, I put on my shade hat and my sunglasses, and walked down through the seemingly deserted hotel and out into the town. Long shadows I didn't recall were plastered on the ground from the new buildings. I asked someone on the street the way to the church. It was like seeing a movie I hadn't seen for years, recollecting the actions only as they happened—here the turn of concourse, there the angle of a store, now crushed between giants. The blackish shade trees were the same and the fence, discolored now like teeth. The church had been fitted with a door that opened as you approached.

I didn't really remember the church after all. Or else it was entirely changed. It had an austere whitewashed frame, through which had been stabbed great wounds of windows, like sliced pomegranates, green angelica and blue ink. The altar cloth was the blue and white I'd seen in Ares, and roses bled over their bowls in the hands of white marble angels with huge open-fan wings of tarnished gilt. A pool of incense hung in the air above the altar, like a mirage. The watch flame flickered in its little crystal canister, showing that God was present. But nobody else was home.

I stood on the tiled floor, staring around, my pulse a drum, searching for the vast scrawled words written in fire on the white wall; SABELLA QUEY IS DAMNED. But there weren't any words, and only the angels with their roses had any connection with Cassi's letter. Surely, there hadn't been marble angels here when momma and I sat among the congregation, tensed for the visitation of light out of or into our souls. Maybe marble angels would come alive, were granted the power of speech.

Their carved faces were frigid over the red flowers like blood. The blank eggs of the eyes stared back at me. Their lips must have parted slowly, and before Cassi's gaze they had stated the truth to her, as she kneeled astonished between the pews. Behold, the mouthpiece of the Lord.

And then one of the angels slowly opened its mouth.

I couldn't believe what I was seeing. I froze, with that feeling of the heart actually turning over which accompanies unpredicted horror. Wider and wider the lips of the angel stretched, as if snarling, as if preparing to bite at me. From out the lips came a huge high-pitched gale of sound, which seemed to split my head apart. Not till the shriek cut off did I scream, irresistibly, but helplessly delayed. The scream sounded far away, and so did the crack of my purse landing on the tiles.

There was a thud, and footsteps. I looked to see the angel running toward me, its mouth pulled wide to bite, but instead there was a man with a distraught face and two gray dog's ears of hair flopping at either side of it.

"Please," said the man, taking my arm, treading on my purse and jumping off it. "Please, don't be alarmed."

"The angel—" I think I said.

"It's just the calliope," said the man.

I looked past him. The angel's mouth remained wide.

"The calliope," said the man. "The organ pipes run up through our angels, there, and when I play they part their lips so they seem to be singing with the congregation. It's rather cute, I suppose. I always run over the hymns at this time. Usually the church is empty. But, oh my, I've really given you a shock, haven't I?"

I felt rather sick and very foolish. I sat down on the edge of a pew and the dog's ears man picked up my purse and put it by me.

He offered me a brandy from the medicine cabinet, but when I refused, he brought me a small tumbler of water instead, from the back room behind the angels.

"And you're a stranger, too," he said. "A newcomer, and now I've frightened you away."

"I'm just passing through," I said. "Some relatives of mine used to come here, years ago."

"That'd be before my time, then. Only been here a year and a half, part-time organist, and museum attendant on the side. If it's that you've come to see, I'm afraid it's not on show today." He seemed to expect a comment.

"Excuse me, what isn't?"

"The museum."

"I didn't know about a museum."

"The museum is generally what visitors to Easterly come in here to see. Or did. One time there was quite some traffic, but once the initial interest died down—Mother Earth gets the original and we get the bits, and everyone forgets. I say museum. I think I overstate."

The water, laying a cold gravitational center through my body, had steadied me.

"I'm sorry, I still don't understand."

"You mean to say, Miss—"

"Holland."

"Miss Holland, you mean to say you didn't know about the archaeological find at Easterly, two years back?"

There it was. It was like a gong booming through

the pit of the world, unheard, detected only by its massive vibration. I still didn't comprehend, yet I recognized the moment.

"What find?"

"Ah, Miss Holland. Are you interested in previous cultures? Are you concerned about the prior civilization of Novo Mars? Don't answer. Let's pretend you are. When they started to process the ground over the river for the New Easterly Complex, they blasted out an old quarry, and straight through it was this blessed confounded hole with a slab in it that dates back a thousand years before the first ships landed here. Just think of it. One thousand years before men started squeaking and picking about over the surface. That's older than the foundations at Dawson, older than the stuff up in the Callicoes. Not only older, but different. That's the real point. *Different.* The news had it, TV newsouts carried it for months. You never heard?"

"I suppose . . . I must have."

Recollect, I never listened to the news of my world, not since my mother died, except those days after I burned Sand Vincent.

"Well, it's a tomb. We've had them before, right? But they're urn burials. And this. This is a sarcophagus. Like the Egyptians on Earth, or the Plutonids—you get me, Miss Holland?"

"Yes."

"Oh, damn it," said the dog's ears man, then he glanced at the altar and said, "Pardon me, Sir. Miss Holland, we've put away the museum for today, but I've nearly scared you half to death. So if you'd *like* to see what we have down there—"

I wanted to say no.

"Yes," I said, "I really would."

He beamed at me.

"Better take off those glasses. The generator runs the lights below, and it's switched to half power now."

I took the sunglasses off, and the wounded window light shattered over me.

"Why, that's strange," said my guide, as he walked

me towards the angels and the room behind, "the very last visitor that came to see the museum—you wouldn't have a brother would you, Miss Holland?"

"No."

"That's strange," he repeated. We went by the angel with the open mouth, and I could see the hairline hinges in its jaw. "A tall man, what I'd call the piratical type. Of course much bigger built than you and black-haired, but you know—a distinct resemblance."

Is he talking about Jace? Do Jace and I look alike? I don't want to think about Jace, now now, nor Cassi, nor anything. They were leveling the ground out there, to create their complex with its ambiguous domes, when they found the hole I had crawled into, and disemboweled it. Whatever they'd found in there, one thing they hadn't found. That thing which seemed to be beating now, like a second crimson heart against my breast.

We were in the organ room, with a door to the robe room, and a static moving stair that led down through a trap in the floor. A notice in the wall said: REPLICATE REMAINS.

"Isn't that too nasty for words?" he asked me, indicating the notice. Then he invited me onto the stair, and pressed the down button. "This used to be the old robe room," he told me. "When they dug up the sarcophagi (or do you prefer 'guses?) it was reckoned the safest storage place in Easterly. Or rather, the safest place that would accept responsibility. Then, after they'd shipped the real relics off to the Federation archives on Earth, the replicas came in here, and here they stayed. Ares wants them, naturally, but we've held out. You know, I do think it would have been kind of nice to have held out all the way. We keep the real articles and have the Federation make the confounded replicas."

Cassi must have come this way, a year ago. Did she see the reality or the replicate? The replicates will be so perfect, I doubt it would have made much difference. Then again, suppose this stone around my neck were in a vault on Earth and a replicate were throbbing on my skin. What difference would *that* make?

As he warned me, the old robe room, now the museum, was dim, and after the rain of sun from the windows I was glad. Along the far wall were a series of blocks, the kind all genuine museums have, to contain and protect the objects inside yet leave them accessible to all around view.

"It's very dark," said my guide. "Of course, the blocks light up. Here we are." He led me, and we stood by the first block in the line, and it came alight like dawn.

The slab across my way in the tunnel, satin-smooth and almost featureless, save that there, there, Sabella, was the crevice you never saw before, only felt, in which your destiny lay like a pebble.

"See that little dinge, just there?" helpfully he pointed. "No one guesses as to what made that pock. You need laser power to cut into such a slab. And look, this next one shows the cut sections."

The second block lit. Inside, the tomb, split wide like a walnut.

My heart rattled. It couldn't beat so fast and let me live.

"And here we are, the insides—"

The third block lights. There it was. Whatever it was. It looked like handfuls of yellow string, and gray wire, and then I perceived a skull that looked to me human, ordinary and simply dead.

"That," he said, "is a Martian. A New Martian. Not dust, but bones. Now, just look at these wrappings from the body—" And he dashed to the fourth block and it lit.

Where the bones had staled, the covering hadn't. It was a sheet of a weave that looked like the best kind of synthetic silk, only a touch faded. The drawing, or maybe embroidery, on the cloth was photographically accurate. A man bent to drink from a cup a woman was handing him. Both were naked, hairless, beautiful. Beside them, stood another man and woman (or rather the first pair, repeated in the fashion of a cartoon), and the woman was kissing the neck of the man. The pictures were very calm, and quite innocent, except for the drop that hung from the woman's throat. These drops are two pieces of crystal, fixed into the design, and the first one colorless as white diamond, the second red.

"The theory is a little grisly, I'm afraid," said my guide. "Do you want to hear it? Originally, there was some outcry over such items being stored under the church if the theory was true, but of course, the safest place for every form of evil is directly under the eye of God. If it is evil."

"I'd like to know the theory."

"Well, first of all, the pictures were taken to mean nothing in particular—domestic duty, affection, between man and woman. Then the visual semantics people got on to it. The idea is that, since only two activities are shown, and quite specifically, they must interrelate. In the first picture, the woman gives the man a cup and he drinks. In the second, the man is giving the woman drink." There was a silence. He glanced at me rather apprehensively. After my outburst at the roaring angel, he wondered if I could take this. "I mean, she is drinking from his neck vein. Which leaves us, if the theorists are correct, with vampirism. Of course, there's nothing supernatural in it. It's probably a rite. We know so little about this people—" He starts to theorize himself, postulating many other acts which the cloth may really be depicting.

I stood, and I called to mind Cassi visiting in momma's house. Cassi not seeming to notice me. Not noticing me till she reread momma's letters, which must have mentioned several things, half hiding, half revealing. Momma, you must have seen the stone, and told her. You must have seen the stone, I know you did, when it was white and when it was red—and yet, even so, for Cassi to make the connection between this replicate under the church, the replicate she thought God led her to see, and myself—

"But superstition is a dreadfully clinging vine," my guide was saying. "The worst moment came for our collection here when the robot digger on the complex unearthed the bones."

I realized something about my guide. Despite his worry over me, which was quite genuine, he'd brought me down here because he felt assured, after my response to the angel, of a sensitive, perhaps hysterical further reaction from me. For months he'd had no custom for this pride of his, this find, and when I screamed in the church, he visualized, somewhere on the dark side of his brain, I might scream a little over these blocks. And so far, I hadn't. So now he was waiting. It was time to speak again.

"You mean there's another burial besides this one?"

"Well, in a way. What I actually meant was that human bones were found in the tunnel, outside the tomb itself."

It didn't register properly. It didn't fit.

"Human bones?"

"Well yes. Something of a mystery, and hence a lot of foolish nonsense, and opposition to us keeping the artifacts of the burial just here. I recall a lady who came all the way from Ares to shout at us. A big name. What was it now—Cooperman—"

"Koberman," I say, before I can hold myself.

"Ah, yes, I believe it was. How did you know?"

"The Kobermans are a big name in Ares."

"I can credit that. This lady now, she spoke a lot about God, and what she owed to Him. She scared me, I don't mind telling you. And as it turned out, her objections were virtually groundless, she didn't even know about the human bones. Then Pennington—he was guide down here then—he blurted it. She went as white as ash, this lady did. That was the first time we had a lady faint in our church, (you were nearly the second). And when she came to, you'd think she'd had some sort of vision. I love my God, Miss Holland, but that sudden turning on, like an electric current, it bothers me. . . ."

I didn't feel anything. No, not quite correct. I felt a sword poised across my neck, delicate as the wing of a butterfly. I couldn't prompt him, but I didn't have to.

"The thing was," he said, "this set of bones the digger unearthed belonged to a perfectly healthy little girl, about eleven years of age, just on the edge of puberty. There was no apparent cause of death, though I'd say she'd crawled in there and maybe the air was bad and she fell asleep and asphyxiated. But that's not good enough for the superstitions of our community. Something had to have lured her in the hole, and killed her. Now who in their senses would agree to that about a tomb full of dead remains?"

I was cold. Christ, I was so cold. Even the roots of my hair, my fingernails, even the moisture in my eyes, cold, cold. . . .

"But who was she?"

"The little girl bones? Well, it's a funny business, I'll admit that. The date of the decay was around eleven or so years before we got them out—they'd sunk back in the earth some, but we can date fairly accurately, even after Martian soil has done its work. But the trouble was, nobody had reported a child missing at that or any subsequent time, here in Easterly. The teeth are the usual way of identifying, and they were a dear little set, all flawless, but for a spot of work on one back molar. So they chased up the dental records in the town, and the only child whose record matched the teeth in the skeleton was a child called—"

Don't. Don't. Don't.

"—Sabella Quey."

He pronounced it Kee. Perhaps that made it all right. Perhaps that means it isn't—can't be—

"But this Sabella Kee (Sabella—that's pretty, don't you think?) Well, she certainly didn't go missing at any point. In fact she and her mother moved out of the area about three years later than the bone-decay date, and went to live over near Brade somewhere, I think the gossip had it, though we never traced them."

No. No.

This man is mad. And he told Cassi all this. And Cassi thought—no wonder Cassi thought—

I went in the tunnel. *I* went in, and *I* came out. I, me, Sabella. Sabella. Oh momma, why aren't you here with me to tell this man he's crazy, and that I'm your daughter, that you slapped and loved and died for.

He was saying something else about the bones, and missing children, and he was moving on and there was one more block, but I didn't want to stay there. I knew now what Cassi heard, what made her hate and fear me, and it was a lie.

But I must, as always, cover my tracks where I can. The tracks of the wolf.

"It's been very good of you—"

"But you must see the last one."

"I'm so sorry, I didn't realize how late—"

And the last block lit up, but I was on the moving stair.

"Come out!" my mother called. "Bel, come out of that, it's nothing but a dirty hole. Bel, do you hear me?"

But that was my dream on the plane to Ares, the dream when Sand woke me, and told me everything was all right. My mother wasn't with me.

But I remember. I *do*.

I was eleven, and nine years before, my father was killed, And I lived in Easterly, and I started to menstruate. And I was unhappy and I walked out of town and I found the tunnel in the quarry, which may have been a metaphor for the vagina, and—

And when I came back to Easterly last night, the house was gone that I'd lived in, and I thought it was as if a chunk of my past had been rubbed out, as if my past were only hearsay, and it suddenly seemed memory itself could be a fake, a fabrication of the mind.

And yet I can remember—

Everything since I came out of the tunnel, clear and absolute and washed with color and pain and shadings.

And everything before I went into the tunnel—yes, I can remember, but—

It's like a diluted painting, or a kind of tableau, where events and people are made of paper and pasted on. . . .

Yes, I know my father died. I know where I lived and where I went to school, and the shape of that room and this tree, and the color of a doll's dress and mother's hair and that it went gray after my father was killed and then she tinted it another color; and I know what my grades were, and when my second teeth came, or maybe a dentist fixing one, and perhaps I climbed trees and perhaps I loved lemon-acid ice cream, but then—

It was just as if I learned those things, the way I learned history dates in school. I could remember, but maybe only—

Second hand.

Outside the church, there was half an hour left of sun. A pink-copper light slicks off the walls beyond the churchyard fence.

Everything seemed to be whirling, the air full of specks, the trees coming undone, everything in shreds, returning to chaos. There was nowhere firm for me to stand, and even my flesh was whirling off, Sabella's flesh that wasn't Sabella's.

And then there was one dark solid, a static beacon in the flood.

The avenger, the dark angel. There was a bar across the street, and he was standing there. He'd been right behind me all the while, right behind this thing he knew wasn't human, not even the part-human thing it thought it was. In the whirling world, only he remained whole, but that was because he was death, just as I always thought.

He'd seen me, but he was waiting for me to cross the street and lie down for the stroke of the sword.

I turned and I ran. By the church and under the shade trees. The path was tiled, and there I could see a back gate and a street beyond.

He'd be running to catch me. He always caught me before. But now I knew what I was, now I was running not only from human vengeance but from my own self, that thing I dreamed in the mirror, its claws sticky with blood, its tongue a black whip, now surely I could run fast enough to get away.

I dropped my purse somewhere. The heel of my shoe twisted and I tore off my shoes and ran on.

I couldn't hear his steps behind me.

My hat was caught in the tree, a black raven. That was funny.

On the street, people got out of my way. Their surprised eager faces flashed past. Perhaps I wasn't running, but the world was dashing away from me, carrying Jace with it.

I ran over a road and a car dived by me, a hot breath of hell on my back. I never turned. I might see death behind me.

Here was a crowd. I ran, I pushed, I was trapped, I was free, I was through.

The sun was going. Try to catch the sun.

Sabella was running. No. Not Sabella. *Something.*

A pain in my side began to slow me, like a piece of lead shot in my vitals. And the red sky was being tipped out over the horizon and overhead the sky was already black.

What place was this? Did I need my fabricated memory, or the real one?

Real one. I was on the highway out of town. Beyond the hypermarkets and the giant stores, where the old beer shop used to be, and where the bars were now like yellow rips in the dark. This was where I was when I was fourteen and the boy with fair hair came by. That's right, that's fine. Full circle. And there was an open-top solar jeep slowing by the walkway.

"Hey, lady!"

Good. That's good. How it has to be.

I turned, and held out my hand, and three grinning human males lifted me into the jeep.

Even death can't outrun this jeep.

Then I looked back.

I couldn't see Jace. The pain was like tears now, like the tears I never did cry, the important ones I held inside me, keeping them, for they were all I had.

The boys in the jeep were laughing, touching my hair, my arms, insidiously my breasts, boldly my knees. They offered me a bottle of wine as the night burst on the front of the windscreen.

Where the plantations of trees ran out from Easterly, they spun the open-top off the road and down a track into darkness. Somewhere in the black they cut the engine and jumped out of the jeep, taking me with them. I didn't have to do a thing, they did it all for me, transported me, put me down, began to strip me.

They were all over me. If I'd have struggled it would have been pointless, but they missed the struggle or some sort of wriggling, panicky response, and so they began to slap me about.

I'd known it. I'm the masochist you suppose me to be. Because I want you to hurt me for what I do to you, I want to expiate my sins with your blows ringing on my flesh. None of this is happening to me. I died, thirteen years back, sitting by a tomb in a hole in a rock.

One of them was sprawled on me, fumbling for the door. His body was hot and wet through his thin clothes, and the other two were rolling on the ground, tugging my arms, yelling. Beyond their heads, I could see stars, as if it mattered. And then the stars went out.

The boy screamed, dragged up and backwards and flung, like a jointless bundle. I could just see his face, the big howling mouth like the mouth of the angel. And then branches crashing, and he was gone. The other two had started up like dogs. I was alone on the ground, but I couldn't really see what was happening. The stars kept going out then reappearing, as shapes went over them. And then one of the boys dropped down beside me, his face turned to mine, snoring wild-eyed through a beard of blood. His fists came scrabbling and were kicked aside, and I heard someone running away through the trees. My night vision had cleared, but I didn't need it any more. I knew the hands of death as they lifted me.

As soon as death touched me, I stopped being afraid. I relaxed totally, and let him carry me, with my clothes hanging off me in portions, and my hair white in my eyes.

There was a hire car parked up on the road. I didn't ask him how he'd got to it in time to come after the jeep. Perhaps he stole the car, perhaps he lost the jeep in any case and found it again merely by luck. It seemed to me that it was inevitable, that he couldn't lose me, he had never lost me.

The car started and he took the wheel. There was a crackle in the cab that must have been his anger, but I didn't look at him.

Then he gunned the engine so the car screamed up the road back to town, and he shouted at me in one long sustained shout. I couldn't hear half the words, and some I heard were off-planet obscenities. It was all distant from me, this shout. Then it stopped and there was silence. Then he said in the flat version of his voice, "Where are you staying?"

"You know everything, but not that?"

"Right."

I told him the location of the hotel, and for a moment I was almost amused. But then I remembered Sabella had died thirteen years ago. Whatever I was, I couldn't be amused.

We drove in silence again.

When we got to the hotel, he drove into the garage, told me to pull my dress together, and then ladled me out of the car and into the foyer and into the lift.

Sabella's head was hurting.

My—Sabella's—arms were bruised.

We went into my room and he shut the door.

He switched on the side lights. He said, "Go in the goddammed shower."

So I went into the shower, and took off the remains

of my clothes, and let the water wash the blood, their blood and mine, off me. And then I put my fingers to the chain around my neck. And I took off the pendant.

I held it in my hand, with the water splashing over my body and through my hair. The stone was paling again, a pale, pale rose.

I stood there, with the water falling on me, staring at the stone, and gradually the water beat me to my knees. I kneeled, and I could only see the stone in my hand, getting paler and paler, as if the life were rinsing out of it.

When Jace opened the cubicle door, I couldn't raise my head from looking at the stone.

"See," I said. "Just like the ghoul lady in the tomb." And then the proper words came, and I said to him, "I'm afraid. I'm afraid," and I couldn't stop saying it, it was the only thing I wanted to say.

He switched off the shower, and came and lifted me. He held me very quietly, and I thought of Sand holding me, rain wet from a shower, but the thought couldn't stay in my brain.

"I'm afraid, Jace."

"I know you are."

The stone was clamped tight in my hand, and my other hand held on to him more tightly. He took me through and put me on the bed, and rocked me. I'd supposed he was going to kill me. But of course he wouldn't. He was like the rest, the lodestone had magnetized him like all the others, and now he was mine. Yet, Jace wasn't like the others. Jace was like, was like—me. No, like Sabella, not like—*me.*

"Why did you want me to see the replicates?" I said.

"You don't know why?"

"Unless—to make me afraid, to—"

"No, Sabella."

"I'm not Sabella."

"You're as much Sabella as you need to be."

"I'm something that killed Sabella, took her form, her skin, her memories—"

"And that's all the memory you have. The human memory. No throwback Martian vignettes?"

I stared at him, at his real face, the only reality. He said, "You didn't see all those Martian blocks, did you?"

"One block I didn't see—"

"There's something I'm going to tell you, Sabella," he said to me. "But not just yet."

He'd stopped looking at my eyes. He looked now at all of me, and as he looked at me, I too began to become real again, alive. When he touched me now it was like fire sponging into me.

"No," I said. But he didn't take any notice of what I said, only of the answer my body was giving back to his hands. "Jace—don't."

"Such a beautiful mouth," he said. "Pity it's a liar."

"You saw me—with the boy in Ares."

"I've seen plenty."

"Jace, I can kill you."

"No."

"Yes I can. Like with the boy. Like Sand. I can, and I don't—I don't want—"

"Forget the others. When did you ever feel this before?"

Damn him, it's true, when did I? But I must fight him, for his own sake—or is it just—

As he raised me, I seemed to be lifted out of myself quite literally, as if my body slipped away and the new body inside rushed free. Then he brought his mouth down over mine very gently and undeniably, and began to kiss me. A wonderful feeling washed through me. It wasn't only sex, which I'd never truly felt before, it was a sensation of peace, of comfort almost. I couldn't fight him. Neither could I fool him. Suddenly I understood I couldn't do a single thing he couldn't handle; I couldn't take from him because he would leave me no space to take, no room for any response but one. Nor need I be ashamed, for I could commit no crime against him, only surrender, give in, let go.

That was what I'd confused with death. That was why I'd been afraid of him.

I was afraid now, but it was a different fear. It wasn't fear at all.

He was beautiful. He had the most beautiful male body I'd ever seen. He was terrible, too, that reality burning like the sun. But I couldn't resist and the sun flamed over me and inside me and I couldn't do a thing. I couldn't even be wise, or try to give him pleasure. I could only take. Take in a new, another way. So this is what they felt, this was what, prolonged, had killed them. Yes—it has the taste of death in it. The great blaze carried me up with it in long gasping leaps of solar energy. And then the world exploded, the sixty-second dawn.

He was lying over me, big golden animal, looking at me with his black, black-lashed eyes half-closed, lazy, amused, tolerant, in control. My fingers ached from grasping him so hard. I dropped the stone, sometime.

I said rather stupidly, with a very human attempt at wit, "Nobody ever gave me a present like that before."

"Relax," he said, "it's Christmas."

He made love to me twice more, before he told me what was in the last museum block. Partly because he wanted me, partly to have that symbol of sexual command clear and definite between us.

In the last block was the other string of bones from the tomb. It had been a double burial, a woman and a man.

The Easterly news archive, like the bars, stayed open all night. It was fully automated, and, because Easterly hadn't yet gained the city sophistry of Ares, there were no human attendants. Jace put me in a booth and dialed the year he wanted. The sheet came up on the screen and it read. TRAGEDY IN COPPER: *One man dead, twenty injured as ore-drill sparks on fire*. It's the year I was—Sabella was—two, the year and the day my father—Sabella's father—died a hundred feet underground in the New Mine, here, at Easterly.

Dressed in our black clothes, as if in mourning, Jace and I were framed by the large white screen. I shifted, disturbed, my body soothed, my mind staring, at odds with each other. "What—"

"Just read down the column."

I read. I read about Sabella's father's death, which left a widow and a two-year old daughter. I read about other injured men and company insurance. Then, at the column's end I read, *Luckier than some, Daniel Vincent, who should also have been at work on the ill-fated drill, had quit work that morning following an altercation with the drill ganger. Vincent, an off-planeter, who has lived in Easterly for five years, also found his luck holding good elsewhere. His twelve-year old son, missing for two days, came home yesterday, alive and well. The Vincents have another son, just one year old today.*

Jace touched the button and the screen went blank. My mind seemed to go blank with it, so when he began to talk to me, I saw what he said in pictures on the that blank brain-screen.

Daniel Vincent brought his family to Novo Mars in the hope of striking rich with the ore boom. But the ore boom, which benefited many, failed Daniel, and in the end, he had to work for the company in Easterly, in order to make up losses. Five years was a long time to Daniel, who was at heart a drifter. A rough, tough hell-raiser of a man, his first son, Jason, bore much of the brunt of Daniel's frustration. The head slaps, the off-hand beatings, were well outside the legal limits of assault, yet, they were brutal enough. They served to convey, more than physical hurt, the unlove that Daniel had for his first son. Then, the second son arrived, and on this second son, belatedly and bizarrely, Daniel fastened a savage possessive affection. If Jason's life was bad before, it got worse in the year which followed. The second son, named Sand for some romantic maybe drunken whim, was the blessing. Jason retained his position as the curse on the Vincent home. Jason ran with a pack of boys, caught in those bouts of hooliganism that plague all colonies once they become townships. Finally, trouble behind and the usual beating ahead, Jason, one sundown, didn't go home. Instead he went climbing in the dry canals outside of town. In an abandoned quarry, his foot kicked through a pile of loosened rocks, eroded by exposure, by time and the moistening of a revitalized atmosphere, and a black pit gaped at him. To Jason, it was a cave to spend the night, a place of shelter. He crawled inside, and when the rock slab blocked his way, he climbed over it to the far side. It was black in the hole, but it seemed like sanctuary.

He stayed in the tunnel, the far side of the tomb slab, one whole night, and the next day he tried to go to Ares, but someone spotted him eventually and brought him home, and Daniel Vincent beat the hell out of him.

A month after the drill fire, Vincent moved off planet. He took his family to Gall Vulcan, and here he periodically deserted his woman and his boys, returning at uneven intervals, like a chronic illness, to pet Sand, and to curse and to beat Jason. He went on spasmodically beating Jason until Jason was fifteen, and then Jason broke Daniel's nose and two of his own fingers. After that, Jace got free, becoming a drifter between the planets, enough of his father in him for that. Sand remained and let the father's petting warp and smear him out of shape in a way Jason had never been warped or smeared by those blunt crusted hands and the belt between them. It had been the father who had rescued Sand, in the beginning, from the blunders he made in his own world of twilight morality and confusion. Later, when Daniel vanished into death, Sand turned incredibly to Jason, and perhaps more incredibly, Jason answered.

Jace had stopped talking and the mind pictures flowed away.

"Sand—" I said.

"No," he said. "Ask me about the tunnel."

I paused, because even in my bewilderment I saw he was asking to be spared any more of Daniel and of Sand. At last I said, "You *made* the tunnel."

"I kicked it open again. It was already made."

"And you never noticed the stone? But all this was ten years before I—"

"We haven't finished with this, yet," he said, and he spun the dial again.

The blank screen lights, and it's last year's newsout, styled quite unlike the earlier crisper bulletin, with capitals that curl, the modern penchant for harking further and further back to the modish past of Earth.

Another skeleton retrieved from the relic tomb cavity. Last night, robot diggers clearing the further debris from the quarry tunnel where last year the unique New Martian tomb slab was discovered, unearthed another mystery find of human bones. These latest ossa, believed to be those of a male around thirteen years of age, are registering as having lain in the tunnel behind the area of the tomb for twenty-odd years or more. Readers will recall the rather uncanny previous disinterment of a prepubescent female skeleton some months ago, identified by dental records as a former Easterly child, still supposed living. There is a possibility no identification, accurate or false, can be made with the latest find, since all teeth are present and perfect and conceivably no dental record exists.

The screen goes out. I can't move. My brain, the blank screen, empty, frozen.

"The Calliope man could have told you about that other parcel of bones," Jace said, "if you'd given him a chance. He likes the buildup gradual." I didn't move. "Come on, Sabella," he said. His voice was slurred, playful, unafraid. "We're in this shit together."

"You're telling me that you're—That you and I—No. You eat and drink and walk in the sun—"

"Sabella, you're missing the sign."

He walked me out of the archive, and across the street into a bar. And then we sat at a table, he with a long glass of golden beer, the very color his soul must be, I thought, I with a glass of strawberry juice, the sort I used to drink in Easterly long ago, pale satin pink, the color the bloodstone goes just before all color fades from it.

If you looked at us, we looked quite normal, and very splendid, very beautiful. You couldn't see my hands shake from where you're sitting, or my heart shake, or my mind.

I didn't believe him, or the newsout, because he was so calm, so uninterested: So, I'm dead. So.

"If you believe this," I said, "I just wish to God I could be like you."

"You don't have to be like me," he said. "I'll be like me for both of us." He took my hand lightly and looked at it, as if my mask of a face with the two distraught eyes in it, might distract him from his purpose. "You're scared," he said, "because you think you're dead. You're not dead any more than I am. We came out of the tunnel, but we didn't go in. Nor did we, you or I, kill those kids that we thought we were all of these years."

"What then? Something killed them."

"Maybe not. Maybe just bits of them got discarded. Or if not, just the shock of being copied. They walked up to a mirror and the mirror came alive. I'd say it was an impulse, a psychic trigger of some kind."

Somehow, words like "psychic" didn't fit in Jace's mouth. He had no gothic approach to any of this, no spiritual anguish. That was what was keeping him on the rails, and me too.

"You mean like a fly-trap plant," I said, "waiting for the first two flies."

He grinned at me. "We're alive. Even you're alive now, Sabella. You can't shoulder the guilt for a crime you don't even remember committing."

"We're *Martians*, then. Why don't we remember back when the place was all bloody lily pillars and damned urns—"

"I don't think it works that way. I think we got made on a blueprint, like two tin cans."

But I imagined the pink indigenous wolves on the hills, their voices, their running to me, and to my kill. They remember, if I don't, what fashioned me, and what I am.

A Martian. An old new reborn Martian. Do I laugh, now?

"Come on," he said, "you've got to live with it. Vampires resurrect, don't they?"

I clenched my hand in his, "But you're not—"

"Come on, baby. You know what I'm supposed to be."

"Before I considered it, I'd snatched my hand away, and half got out of my chair. But he took my hand back and I sat down again.

I said feverishly, "There are too many coincidences. It's absurd. Even to Cassi spotting Sand's name in an ad, and recalling it from Easterly small-town gossip, which I guess is what happened. Or am I to assume the coincidences are deliberate. This planet dragging its survivors together again."

Jace said, "If my goddam bastard of a father had stayed on in Easterly, you might not have had to make such a ballsup of your life till now."

"Stop patronizing me," I said. "All right, you know how to lay me. It doesn't give you the right to treat me like a child."

"That's the way I have to treat you," he said. "At least for now. And you sure as hell know why."

"No," I said.

But he stood up, drained the gold beer with swift gold undulations of the throat muscle that fascinated me, because I was reducing everything to detail, minutiae. Then he led me out of the bar.

On the street, he said to me, "For Christ's sake, Bella, I'm not afraid of you."

"I am. *I* am. You don't know—"

"I can turn you out like a light," he said. "Any time at all. And that's all you need tell yourself."

In the lift I started to shiver convulsively while the tinny music played. By the time we got to my room, I could hardly walk.

He sat on the bed and took me on his lap, and for all I'd cried I wasn't a child, I was glad enough to rest there in his arms. And I thought of Sand's descriptions—Jace the defender, the rock, Jace the comforter. And I wondered if these stories of Sand's were true, and still I didn't know just what love there had been between them, or hate, or if love could cancel all hatred, hatred all love.

Presently, Jace showed me the stone, which I'd left lying, and which he'd picked up.

"See," he said gently. "Meant for you, not for me. The infallible meter. You're almost out of gas."

"I can't."

But he moved my head until my mouth was against his throat, and easily he lay back and pulled me with him.

"Do it," he said.

So I did.

Instinct. And then, more than instinct. It isn't the same. Not the old thing, the sense of breathing, it's more than that, it's—but I can't say, I don't have the words to say. It isn't performed during love, that's a snare for enemies, the robber's way, the fool's way. But it's an act of love, nevertheless. And for the first time, I could kill a man only by excess of this, the drawing from the vein, the milking of life, and I would kill him out of love, not need. I could kill him then, but he said to me quietly, "That's it, Sabella," and I heard, and I wanted to leave him, but oh, I couldn't leave him, couldn't—and then he put his hands on my shoulders, and with his strength which was always greater than mine, just as he was generally a fraction swifter, he lifted me from him and held me away, and when the film of the great silence of the well I had been drinking at seeped off me, and my eyes unglazed, he put me down beside him, and for a while, we were quiet, as if after the other act of love.

"What," I said to him at last, "did you feel?"

"You kissing me," he said. "Very nice."

"But you can control it. You can stop me."

"Anytime."

"Even if I took when we were making love?"

"You won't."

"But if I did?"

"Try it," he said. "You won't sit on your ass for a month."

The stone was a drop of ruby in his hand, and he gave it back to me.

I was not afraid any more.

I believe in God. I think I believe in Jesus Christ. That night in Ares, I knelt, and I begged someone who was above bargaining to help me, And see, I was helped.

I've thought about it, and I have a conclusion to offer, though Jace doesn't care about it. It's a fact for him, insane but self-demonstrating. I am a woman he wants, and I want him, and he'll haul me with him to other worlds, or stay awhile here on this world which I perceive is ours, and which he takes as a stop-over point or a returning point, but which emotionally he views as just another hotel in space. Which makes me wonder if we are, in a way, still those two children who wandered into the grave-tunnel, not just exact copies of their bodies and their memories and their names. Certainly, we have no recollection of a past to set archaeologists and spiritualists squalling and turn the Revivalist Church on its ear. The last impulse of two lovers in a last lost tomb, that's what formed us, and what pins us together, beyond sex and trauma and loneliness and need. We're utterly unlike, opposed, embattled. We can fight all we want, and we do fight. But this nail passes through both of us, a bolt of light as in a picture of Mars, piercing, but not breaking, the vessels of glass we are. Which to Jace is an idea to laugh at, the same as to liken him to earth, and fire.

And for the conclusion? It's all unround.

Before the Earth ships landed, started up their colonies, pumped oxygen into the air and water over the ground and planted things, acting like God in Eden, this planet was four-fifths dead. But before death came, what changes had occurred among a people who raised lily pillars and sealed death in an urn, a people whose technology was either so incredible or so obsolete that men can find no trace of it? I think when all but half the stores of the world were gone, they happened on, or evolved deliberately, a method of sharing. Of the little water and the little food there was, one would eat and drink, and when he was strong, the other would take from him the vital element which food and drink had made—his blood. So there were those who lived by feeding on the things of the earth, and those who lived by feeding upon *them*. It's a situation that admits no intolerance. A system that requires a careful pairing, a creation of partners, who could permit in love what could never be permitted in hate or greed. Except that some were greedy or reluctant, forcing, taking, pillage and robbery, and so the process of seduction followed, the murderous snare I had practiced, not knowing, (or could it be remembering?) another way. That destroyed them, or else, ultimately the planet had nothing left to give, even in half-shares. So the lovers had their tomb, and after them dust again filled all the urns.

It doesn't frighten me anymore about the tomb, the possession Cassi set out to destroy, the possession which is me. And Jace, if she had known. As for guilt, I still feel it, I'm still culpable, but it's become a familiar thing, a piece of me, no more. Because guilt is purposeless. I can undo nothing. Yet in the future, I can live without destruction. And more than that, simply, I can live.

We went to Hammerhead and tidied the house, heard the occasional cicadas and walked on the hills. Once three wolves came out in the dusk and briefly followed us, gilded by stars and blazoned with eyes. Jace whistled them and they came to him. To him they're dogs. He would have thrown them a stick, I think, but they loped away before it occurred to him.

And yet, by that hole of a grave he dug for Sand, I've seen him stand in the sunlight, while I linger in the shade. I've seen his face, closed; I've seen him recall his life as a human man, knowing he is no longer that.

We won't stay here forever, or even very long. I've never seen another planet. This is all I know. I tell him we're the last New Martians, and he says sure, baby, forgetting graves, his light to my dark, his wide outward gaze to my introspection.

But we're not human. No humans are as we are.

The last Martians.

He has to dominate me, that's essential; for I take his life's blood. The victim must be stronger than the oppressor—or he dies. He has to tell me when and how, and where to walk, and if I may, and I obey him, but that's not for always. I've been anchorless for years. I've wanted a discipline beyond myself, and needed it to show me how to master myself, and I'm learning this too, he's teaching me. In the end, maybe I shall be the one to say that this planet is where we return to and where we remain.

And maybe the planet is a vampire too, taking from the life that moves over it, waiting for its resurrection from the deadness of a desert before it whispered to its inner dead in their obscure burial places, Come, rise up, taste of the oxygen in the skies, and the poured out waters, and the spilled dreams of men.

Men don't own this world. And though the Federation of Earth leaves only replicates behind it, the bloodstone between my breasts is real. I'm not a woman in the human sense. A taker of blood, I don't squander that gift at quarter season. But still it seems to me that I may not be infertile. This traveling man who has saved me, might not be of one mind with me as he blows between the stars, but I can hear destiny now in the whistling cry of the enduring wolves, the cry of survival. There may come a time that whatever brought us together will shout for its purpose to be fulfilled through us, the last of our kind.

You will have noted I must still walk in shadows, I'm still closer to the dark, the secret, the mystery. Don't think me Jace's slave, for if you do, you miss all truth in what I've told you, and you miss the promise that one day I may choose to make this man the father to our planet's children.

And on that day, or night, the last shall be first.

Presenting MICHAEL MOORCOCK
in DAW editions

The Elric Novels

☐	ELRIC OF MELNIBONE	(#UW1356—$1.50)
☐	THE SAILOR ON THE SEAS OF FATE	(#UW1434—$1.50)
☐	THE WEIRD OF THE WHITE WOLF	(#UW1390—$1.50)
☐	THE VANISHING TOWER	(#UW1406—$1.50)
☐	THE BANE OF THE BLACK SWORD	(#UW1421—$1.50)
☐	STORMBRINGER	(#UW1335—$1.50)

The Runestaff Novels

☐	THE JEWEL IN THE SKULL	(#UW1419—$1.50)
☐	THE MAD GOD'S AMULET	(#UW1391—$1.50)
☐	THE SWORD OF THE DAWN	(#UW1392—$1.50)
☐	THE RUNESTAFF	(#UW1422—$1.50)

The Oswald Bastable Novels

☐	THE WARLORD OF THE AIR	(#UW1380—$1.50)
☐	THE LAND LEVIATHAN	(#UW1448—$1.50)

The Michael Kane Novels

☐	CITY OF THE BEAST	(#UW1436—$1.50)
☐	LORD OF THE SPIDERS	(#UW1443—$1.50)
☐	MASTERS OF THE PIT	(#UW1450—$1.50)

Other Titles

☐	A MESSIAH AT THE END OF TIME	(#UW1358—$1.50)
☐	DYING FOR TOMORROW	(#UW1366—$1.50)
☐	THE RITUALS OF INFINITY	(#UW1404—$1.50)
☐	THE TIME DWELLER	(#UE1489—$1.75)

If you wish to order these titles,
please see the coupon in
the back of this book.

Recommended for Star Warriors!

The Novels of Gordon R. Dickson

- ☐ DORSAI! (#UE1342—$1.75)
- ☐ SOLDIER, ASK NOT (#UE1339—$1.75)
- ☐ NECROMANCER (#UE1481—$1.75)
- ☐ HOUR OF THE HORDE (#UE1514—$1.75)
- ☐ THE STAR ROAD (#UJ1526—$1.95)

The Commodore Grimes Novels of
A. Bertram Chandler

- ☐ THE WAY BACK (#UW1352—$1.50)
- ☐ TO KEEP THE SHIP (#UE1385—$1.75)
- ☐ THE FAR TRAVELER (#UW1444—$1.50)
- ☐ THE BROKEN CYCLE (#UE1496—$1.75)

The Dumarest of Terra Novels of E. C. Tubb

- ☐ INCIDENT ON ATH (#UW1389—$1.50)
- ☐ THE QUILLIAN SECTOR (#UW1426—$1.50)
- ☐ WEB OF SAND (#UE1479—$1.75)
- ☐ IDUNA'S UNIVERSE (#UE1500—$1.75)

The Daedalus Novels of Brian M. Stableford

- ☐ THE FLORIANS (#UY1255—$1.25)
- ☐ CRITICAL THRESHOLD (#UY1282—$1.25)
- ☐ WILDEBLOOD'S EMPIRE (#UW1331—$1.50)
- ☐ THE CITY OF THE SUN (#UW1377—$1.50)
- ☐ BALANCE OF POWER (#UE1437—$1.75)
- ☐ THE PARADOX OF THE SETS (#UE1495—$1.75)

If you wish to order these titles,

please use the coupon in

the back of this book.

DAW presents TANITH LEE

"A brilliant supernova in the firmament of SF"—**Progressef**

☐ **THE BIRTHGRAVE.** "A big, rich, bloody swords-and-sorcery epic with a truly memorable heroine—as tough as Conan the Barbarian but more convincing."—*Publishers Weekly.* (#UW1177—$1.50)

☐ **VAZKOR, SON OF VAZKOR.** The world-shaking saga that is the sequel to THE BIRTHGRAVE . . . a hero with super-powers seeks vengeance on his witch mother. (#UJ1350—$1.95)

☐ **QUEST FOR THE WHITE WITCH.** The mighty conclusion of Vazkor's quest is a great novel of sword & sorcery. (#UJ1357—$1.95)

☐ **DEATH'S MASTER.** "Compelling and evocative . . . possesses a sexual explicitness and power only intimated in myth and fairy tales."—*Publishers Weekly.* (#UJ1441—$1.95)

☐ **NIGHT'S MASTER.** "Erotic without being graphic . . . a satisfying fantasy . . . It could easily become a cult item. Recommended."—*Library Journal.* (#UE1414—$1.75)

☐ **DON'T BITE THE SUN.** "Probably the finest book you have ever published."—Marion Zimmer Bradley. (#UE1486—$1.75)

☐ **VOLKHAVAAR.** An adult fantasy of a man who sold his soul for total power—and the slave girl who became his nemesis. (#UE1539—$1.75)

☐ **THE STORM LORD.** A Panoramic novel of swordplay and of a man seeking his true inheritance on an alien world. (#UJ1361—$1.95)

DAW BOOKS are represented by the publishers of Signet and Mentor Books, THE NEW AMERICAN LIBRARY, INC.

THE NEW AMERICAN LIBRARY, INC.,
P.O. Box 999, Bergenfield, New Jersey 07621

Please send me the DAW BOOKS I have checked above. I am enclosing $__________ (check or money order—no currency or C.O.D.'s). Please include the list price plus 50¢ per order to cover mailing costs.

Name ________________________

Address ________________________

City __________ State __________ Zip Code __________

Please allow at least 4 weeks for delivery